ROLAND MULDOON was born in Weybridge, Surrey, in between air-raid warnings. He left school in 1956 and worked in many jobs, ranging from Brixham fish sorter to chainman on the new Victoria line. He studied Stage Management at the Bristol Old Vic Theatre School. It was in this city that he teamed up with life-time partner/wife, Claire. In 1963 they joined the Unity Theatre before setting up the legendry underground theatre group CAST. Eventually they had two children, which has led so far to two grandchildren. In 1980, Roland received a Village Voice OBIE award for his one-man play, "Confessions of a Socialist". In 1981, CAST created a New Variety circuit in London featuring a new wave of comedy. In 1986, the group took over the iconic Variety Theatre, the Hackney Empire. When they parted company with the Empire in 2005, they left behind a fully refurbished theatre. Roland co-starred in the US movie "Bucharest Express". He is currently writing his Hackney Empire memories, "Taking on the Empire", as well as helping setting up www.newvarietylives.co.uk.

The White Van Papers

Tales of London Today:
Bugs, Murder and Privilege

Roland Muldoon

authorHOUSE®

AuthorHouse™ UK Ltd.
500 Avebury Boulevard
Central Milton Keynes, MK9 2BE
www.authorhouse.co.uk
Phone: 08001974150

First published by AuthorHouse 6/14/2011

ISBN: 978-1-4567-7945-0 (sc)

In memory of Marcia Zena Lawes

For Claire, Laura Jane, Alison, Ruby and Lucia

And with thanks to Aldous Eveleigh, Ernest Dalton, Gareth Wagland, John Vice and Neil Hedger

Much more is revealed to the two
token cops sitting on their bums than
they imagined. But it takes others to
open the files for them.

Amidst murder, torture, organized
crime and the Olympics, who
is listening and who is seeking
revenge? Who is killing who?

April 2012

My name is Frank Donahue. I'm a mostly out-of-work journalist, exiled for want of cash in Chingford on the edge of Epping Forest. Some time ago I began receiving nudges (for want of a better word) that something in the vicinity of where we live 'would be of great interest to me'. The cryptic message – at least that's what I first thought it was – read:

'Wiltshire plumber, packed with insight, key under Venus'.

As a journalist as near to skid row as I ever wanted to be, I felt I didn't need to be teased by a crossword nut - one who I have quite probably worked with in one of my previous newspapers posts. Perhaps some kind soul was trying to re-engage me back into normal life by setting me some kind of a task. 'What kind of helping hand is that?' I asked the dog. Had the news of our dire financial straits become that public? Or was it a job I was being offered? I chose the moment to ask my better half, as a crossword buff, if the clue meant anything to her. Her unkindly snarl helped me put the whole tease out of my mind for some time.

The long-heralded web changes for the future of the newspaper industry were now becoming all too apparent. With my grim prospects in mind, it seemed that navel gazing had become my preferred daily routine. Unemployment felt to me like I was giving up on life itself. I was in danger that I might just stop trying.

It was a whole month later, walking the avenues and

byways of Chingford, kicking a ball for my fat, reluctant dog, that I noticed an old builders' van, parked off the road, picking up loads of threats of removal notices. There it was: the clue I wasn't looking for. Painted on the side of an ageing Ford van was the inscription, 'Theo Snowden Wiltshire's 24-Hour Emergency Plumbers'. Okay, nothing ventured, nothing gained: I cleaned the grimy passenger window and could just make out boxes of files and other assorted packages stacked inside. It came to me like a shot. In our garden we have a statue of Diana the goddess of hunting. Hardly Venus but nevertheless a classical statue of a naked woman with concrete tits and a moss-covered curvy bum. Sure enough, under the statue I found the vehicle's keys.

It's a wonder the van had survived so long without being towed away. I can only suppose it was the words '24-Hour Emergency Plumbers' and being parked up on a grass verge in a non-restricted zone that confused the parking authorities into uncustomary leniency. Still, we were lucky, if that's the right word - in more prosperous times Waltham Forest Council felt obliged to clear the streets as soon as day broke.

About the same time that I discovered the records, files and video tape, I received the first of four e-mails from Gus Redknapp, a sub-editor hanging on to his job at The Guardian. He had been 'officially' asked if I was still working on Home Office stories. Originally I had written on the case of Delroy Denton, a Home Office and Customs and Excise controlled 'plant' who brutally murdered three women and to this day remains in a British prison. More recently, I knocked out an article for Gus on the continuing practice by the bashful authorities of using foreign stooges, speculated on the composition of the 'plants' and queried their current whereabouts and use.

At first I thought that it might be good news from Redknapp, yet I pondered the word 'officially'. The Metropolitan Police hadn't been pleased with my efforts in the past. The next message read like another puzzle. 'What's your link with the Land of OZ?' It took me some time to work that one out. Then came, 'I keep being asked what you are up to these days' followed by 'Must plod on'. I got it - 'plod' as in the Met. In the middle of the night I forced myself to actually get up and go and start the plumbers' van.

The battery was totally flat and it took the RAC man ages to arrive and quite some time to get the sad old van running again. Despite having no insurance or road tax and without telling anyone we were going, the dog and I drove slowly through Epping Forest and, by-passing the M25, took the van to my wife's cousin's farm near Aylesbury and there under the trees, in a misty dawn in a flat field, I left it. The van contains records and loads of video footage, all from the first half of 2010, around the time of the General Election. As the implications build I still hesitate to publish. I have laid the records out for you to read - they are in chronological order. What its importance is and where it will lead I am still not certain. The jury is out, as they say. But what to do?

This is how they came to me. The first item appears to be the transcript of a conversation between two detectives in a stake-out car in London in the spring of 2010. One is male and middle aged - I expect he is ready for retirement and quite probably a Detective Sergeant of long standing – and the other female, somewhere in her thirties, recently seconded from a parking division and now I imagine is a Detective Constable. The 'records' below are presented in the order that they came to me.

Items

Here we go

1. Thwaite/Murray recording transcripts

March 2010

Transcript 1

Police Detective David Thwaite speaks first in this and all later transcripts. Then PC Patricia Murray speaks and one after the other it continues throughout this part of the 'records'

"Steak out at the stake out... You have left your stuff on my seat again. Move it and I'll pass you yours. Hurry up it's cold out here and your double burger with cheese is getting colder."

"Cheers!"

"No cheese …While I was away, did anything happen?"

"You must be joking."

"Steak out at the stake out?"

"You must have done that a hundred and one times. If only it was true."

"Nothing happened then?"

"This horrible and greasy and cold plastic tray is making me an even fatter woman, as I eat this cardboard meat for the umpteenth time. I'm challenging my already challenged figure. That's what's happening, so cheers."

"Well, mine is without the cheese and the only taste is the gherkin."

"That's because I expect you're a tight arse, saving pennies."

"Better than being a fat arse... So what happened next?"

"I will let that pass...About the boy who was pushed from the roof, or the funeral in Willesden?"

"Whichever... Your Auntie Yvonne's funeral, then."

"Well, Yvonne was called 'Auntie' by many, well known in the community and get this, she was a paid-up coppers' nark, the proper business, wore fancy hats at church and all that. She started out as a local gossip, told everyone about everyone else's secrets, the brethren finally played a game of Chinese whispers with her. You had to laugh. Sometimes it got nasty though. People would deliberately distort what they told her, for one reason or another. Then they would find themselves falling out with each other, when they heard back what was now being said, by her no less, about themselves. If you get my meaning, she had power."

"How?... Why where and when?"

"Shut up let me get on with it, Just living within a mile of Roman Road it would be hard not to get sucked in, everything is on tap. it don't matter what race you are, there's a taste on offer. It's the myth of the place. It's in a league all on its own and let me tell you it's hard for me living near there, with my kids and doing this job, so I keep my mouth tight. They think I'm still in traffic, parking or something. It's hard to refuse the tit bits, know what I mean? ...Anyway Yvonne told us all that she knew who was around when the boy got shoved."

"Us, that's a laugh, you do mean the Met... don't you?"

"I am trying to be brief."

 "What's that got to do with the Roman Road?"

"It's where I was told that Auntie Yvonne had been killed, murdered."

"Is that significant?"

"I think that a lot of the boys on the local tower block roof were connected with her death; somehow. If some of them had got time in the nick because of her, for what some other dumb kid had done…and some did, there would have been a feeling of vengeance towards her. This was before the Murder Mile shootings hit the press and the hoody knife thing took off big time. The dumb kid who did the pushing wasn't protected and incidentally nobody has heard from him since. Get my meaning on this one. Anyway to cut a long story short I went to Auntie's funeral last week."

"Last week? Only last week…! I see what you mean... I thought you said the incidents were some time ago."

"They were. I'm filling in the picture. If you ain't going to listen I shan't bother to talk."

"Okay, I am interested. What happened at the funeral then?"

"I was late and there was other funerals going on. I got lost and was feeling all hot and bothered, when I saw them. I stood there and watched them coming up the main path in a procession following the coffin which had a huge 'Auntie Y' sign and flowers all over the place and in the crowd were boys from the tower block, well that's who I guess they are. I know some of their parents. I went to school with their mums. There were some Africans and some well known Hackney whites as well."

"Social workers types?"

"No wider than that. I'm not certain that there wasn't anyone from the Met though. You would have thought they would turn up after all the help she gave them. Some of the youth were finding it hard to be serious. When I finally got to the grave, some old timers, who I didn't recognise, wearing their best suits, as is the custom back home, filling in the grave with shovels, got themselves covered in mud. When I looked round the mixture of wayward locals had slipped off. Later on, at the wake in the Polish Club oddly enough none of them lot were anywhere to be seen. Me and the kids was there and a few others I didn't know. I heard later that the local youth eventually turned up, team handed, just as the hall was closing and somehow persuaded the Polish caretaker to let them stay open till dawn, the rascals charged an entrance fee, would you believe, turned the place into some kind of party with DJs and live acts."

"So you think Auntie Y or whatever her name is, got done away with?"

"Pass me your bag."

"I'm still drinking my coffee."

"The back seat is full of junk, your newspapers, food bags. Do you have to keep your travelling bag there? All the time?"

"Well, as even you are aware, we are not supposed to draw attention to ourselves, and an untidy back seat looks normal."

"I thought you said the other day that sometimes it seems that drawing attention to ourselves might be our only role."

"It is funny to think that the cameras are watching us, watching some one else."

"Do you think they want to see if we clear out your rubbish from the back seat?"

"Guess that they're running a book on who will do it."

"They would bet, I would do it, because I'm the woman."

"If they were even interested in us."

"If it wasn't for the overtime...You said the other day that it was to get away from Jennifer."

"Well, I shouldn't have."

"How does she feel about us spending ten sometimes twelve hours cooped up together?"

"She doesn't let it enter her mind."

"What's the travel bag for, then?"

"Well, seeing as you must know... And here is the plain truth. Sometimes I plan to do a runner... Each time I've thought, that's it, I have had enough, I find myself with self-created obstacles. It might be that we are expecting some people or the kids are being surprisingly friendly all of a sudden. And I think twice. Just when I've reached the end of the road someone is nice to me...So I packed my bag for the time when I should quit the scene and I can't give myself an excuse."

"It's been here for at least two days."

"I'm frightened of losing the job, if you must know."

"Look there is movement....at last."

"Where?"

"Over there in the car park...Is that Bob Crow?"

"I expect so, that must be his briefcases he's taking out of the boot. Our briefing pic is from the same angle... look."

"Who is he anyway?"

"What? You were at the Briefing weren't you? He is the leader of the RMT the rail workers union. Note the time down in to your record pad."

"Even I know that."

"And he looked round. Do you think he spotted us?"

"Hope so."

"What's his game? Why are we here?"

"Does it matter? He's probably threatening another tube strike. In fact I think it's a rail strike. He's a proper East End man, cocky too, thinks before he replies. I saw him on telly. They asked how could he justify at a time of economic crisis that his members get a six hundred quid a week basic and he said, 'Seven hundred'."

"More than us then, let's face it can't get any lower, rock bottom basics, like it or lump it...so why are we here?"

"I don't know... It could even be that we are protecting him.....from who knows what."

"It must be time to clock off soon. You can drop me round the back of Hackney Town Hall and I will walk the rest."

"That will do you good... I 'm not sure what Jennifer is up too, who she spends her time with. It could be the priest, she sees a lot of him, or her much younger half brother who is always hanging about, or who knows a wandering gypsy, but I keep getting clues , just little things, two cups even two glasses and she says that she has been on her own all day."

"Do you get gypsies in that part of Acton?"

"There are some permanently camped under the A40."

"Have you seen a disproportionate rise in the stock of clothes pegs?"

"If I had said that you would have said I was racist... stereotyping."

"Perhaps we should stake her out... anyway ... I'll get out here.. Thanks and goodnight."

"Yeah, see you."

Recording transcript 2

"You have a look of concern about you."

"Well…When I left you, behind the Hackney Empire I walked down Sylvester Path and at the end of the passage I saw three youngish men, standing in the middle of the path and looking straight at me. As I got up close one of them said out loud, 'She was at the funeral.' So I said what of it? And the tall light-skinned one said that he knew I worked for the Police. That worried me I can tell you, as it's no secret that there are longstanding bad feelings between the Police and the black community, going way, way back. I bet you even knew. Back to the killing of Colin Roach and lots more incidents. It's a well known fact, they put new recruits into Hackney, let them speed around at breakneck speeds. They shot an old Paddy carrying a plastic bag a couple of years back. They behave like arrogant arseholes as they get trained up. If things get serious they are seen, quite honestly, as the enemy. The community closes up, tight. Okay, fear of reprisals stops some from speaking up, I will grant you, but it's mostly because of the basic hard learnt lack of trust in the Hackney Police Force. Anyway the young African-looking one stood a few paces back as if he was a look out. So I asked them straight out what did they want and at the same time I kept walking. Cos to tell you the truth I was shitting myself. Although it's not common to mug black women, it's usually young 'uns that do that, I was very apprehensive to put it mildly. 'Are you a policewoman? I have been told you are,' said the intelligent-looking one. They already had stated that

I was so there was no point in not answering. 'What of it?' I said. 'Well,' said the bright one, 'we would like to ask you something.' 'Did you know I was coming home this way?' I asked them back.

'Shut up' said the tall one. Don't you dare to speak to me like that I said and pushed along until I got into the bright lights of Mare Street. When I got outside the KFC I turned to face them. 'What is it you want? Spill it out.' The tall one said, 'Why was you at that funeral thing?' I said that it was nothing to do with him, and the other one asked why was I watching them and not joining in. I said 'Actually I was late and trying to catch up.' The little one then said 'cos I was fat and do you know I swung out without thinking what I was about and grabbed him by the ear hole. The others laughed at him. And - you won't believe this - at that very moment, out of the blue a squad car whooped up, lights flashing and two officers jumped out almost before you could say Jack Robinson, they had them in the back of their car. All I got was a reassuring palm of the hand from the driver and they were gone."

"They must have been watching them."

"My heart rate was pumping, I had to hold onto the street railings to get my cool back."

"Well, anything more?"

"Hang on. I haven't told you all yet. As I walked home, just near where the original Tesco's was. The first one ever was near Well Street."

"I know where you mean. Go on."

"The patrol car came up silently behind me and the driver lowered his window and asked was I alright and did I want a lift. The last thing I want to be seen doing is getting out of a police car in my neighbourhood. I said it's only a few streets away and I need the air, and he said, '94 McCafferty House, isn't it?'"

"What happened to the three guys?"

"They said they had had a word with them and they won't bother me again and with that responded to a call and zoomed off."

"Well, that was lucky."

"Was it though? I mean, the driver knew my address. They didn't acknowledge that I was an officer."

"Well, here we are, and for whatever reason those above have, we are in full view outside our Mr Crow's house...I will position us over there. And you note time and all that bollocks."

"Okay then. I mean to get forty winks, I spent half the night arguing with my sister about it all. She started on about why I was still in the service and how. Because I had put my hand up at school, it was all my own fault for always seeking approval. Because my dad was so strict, we had found it impossible for us to do anything different. So I, according to her had just conformed all my life blah, blah. How come I couldn't hit a note yet was still singing in the church Youth Choir even when I was twenty eight, How our Dad ruled our lives, banning our boyfriends, 'Mister Respected in the Community' had apparently been caught out when I had suddenly announced - just to outdo him, according to her, mind you - 'Well, I'll join the Police then'. He couldn't say nothing against it, he was claiming out loud in public to be Mr Community, a righteous pillar of the integrated and ever-so-respectable Black Community. Now that he has gone, she claimed, I should chuck it in and get a respectable job with Hackney Council, or down at the dole office or something that don't worry the neighbours. She didn't mind looking after the kids. On top of all that she complained that I didn't speak much when I'm at home because I spent all day talking to you. I pointed out the overtime came in handy and how we couldn't count on her always being on some government training initiative. And when she finally come out with 'I was putting on weight sitting in a car all day.' You know the truth hurts. It can you know. Anyway we finally made up, you know, cried in each other's arms and got to bed around dawn. I didn't need all that. So that's enough of me. What did he do? Bob Crow. What is he really known for? Why are we here? The briefing was so quick and they didn't say much. It was as if it didn't matter, just a detail."

"It's as I told you yesterday ...I think I did. His main claim to fame is that he gets the rail and tube workers out on strike. And it seems that he is some kind of born again Communist. He's on telly a lot, I heard him say screw you in a polite sort of way to the rail management on a number of occasions, I also know that he is a supporter of Millwall. I think I got it wrong the other day when I said £700 not £600 he might have said £50 grand not £40 grand a year for some staff. I don't care why we are here, it's enough me that we are."

"I should have become a train driver."

"Why don't you doze off now?"

Recording transcript 3

"So, off we go …again."

"Where did you first meet Jennifer then?"

"Oh, you're awake then? Boy do you snore."

"Sorry, but it's done the trick….ooh … let me stretch … Oh, we're moving… Where are we going?"

"Home, they clocked us off…. My relationship with Jennifer is something I don't like to talk about, until quite recently, actually. But now I've been thinking everything over. You know, as you do every now and again, well I do anyway. I might as well start with you, seeing as we haven't anything else to talk about. And I haven't worked out my - our - past as a story; before….. But it is one, not one of great importance, but it is my one."

"Go on then. Open up?"

"She really is good looking, well quite good looking and very bright. Better read than I am. She is reading a book currently about modern French philosophy. I can't keep up and I don't really want to. We met in Glasgow when I was an undercover plod in the early eighties. Because I could pass as working class I was told to get a job in Scotland and joined the Socialist Workers Party the SWP. Have you heard of them?"

"Maybe."

"There was some serious ones planning the coming revolution and some just getting stoned at the weekends.

My job was nothing more than to go along with what was being asked of us ordinary members, with not too much enthusiasm, even sell the paper, every now and again, collect the names involved and receive their internal info and pass it on…. I had to sell the Socialist Worker paper. One week it had the banner headline 'IT'S ALL LIES' – of course they were talking about something that the then Tory Government had said. I felt such a nerd. Passers-by actually laughed. I was the most diligent, sold the most - it made me popular in the branch. Anyway, I put myself about. I could do it, join in and agree with most of what was being said. That's when I met her. Everyone wanted to have it off with Jennifer. No one took the piss out of her name, or that she was a bit posh. They took the piss out of me because I was English, but not her though. I do believe even your would-be international and socialist-educated Scots quite regularly hate us; and the southern English men particularly."

"Was it love at first sight?"

"In those days everyone was fucking everyone. At first when she seemed to pick me, I thought it was because having one regular bloke would help to keep the predators at bay. But it wasn't that. It was that she too was undercover."

"She was also what you called an undercover plod?"

"No."

"What then?"

"She was into something much more important than I

was. I was her cover. What she actually got up to, was getting friendly with this guy from the IRSP; the Irish Republican Socialist Party'. He claimed that he had fired a machine gun over the roofs of West Belfast at the Army when the troubles first got started. He was exciting and it was infectious …and our Jennifer led him on. I never believed him; it all sounded wishful thinking to me. At the same time she was also pretending to be flirting with a high-up Tory MP. Suddenly it came out in the press that he, the Tory, was a Republican target. Even though I don't believe he was. The shit hit the fan. There was a lot of embarrassment and she was forced to lie at an internal MI5 investigation. They made her claim that the Tory was indeed the target, that she was all along keeping tags on our token Irishman and why she was having it off with him. They interned the poor bastard. After all he was claiming to know those who did assassinate people. I don't think he actually did. He struck me as too frightened to get really involved, on the edge of things, just hanging out with us showing off….So she left the police force and I was stuck in Glasgow."

"Selling the Socialist Worker?"

"Jennifer took up counselling. She became a qualified counsellor. I was relieved from the Glasgow duties. I was a bit sad about that you know. I liked a lot of the people and then again at the same time, I was reporting on them. At the same time I was agreeing with what they were saying; paid to do that, I was shopping them. It was enough to turn me into a schizophrenic. Jennifer got pregnant and I know that they're mine, in case you're wondering, the twins, unfortunately for them, look more like me then her. Anyway I was told to drop out of the Revolution, sell what was called student hashish, and to introduce a proper trained infiltrator in my place."

"They hadn't sussed that you was a pig?"

"Thank you. I suppose that would be the language they would have used. No they hadn't and I don't believe they ever did and my successor became a legend, he famously diverted union donations away from the 1984-85 Miners' Strike."

"Oh yes I remember the miners' strike. We used to put money in their buckets every weekend. I've seen people put food in the collection bucket, they stood outside Tesco's. What! Do you mean that stuff was going to the Police all along?"

"I doubt it but I don't know - it went on for a year and a bit. Most of the collections must have been getting though. You know the schizoid thing. I put in the bucket. I couldn't trust Thatcher and yet people loved her. That's schizoid too."

"Then?"

"We were moved to Bristol. I was virtually a chauffeur working at Cheltenham GCHQ. I'm not allowed to say any more than that. You're not allowed to mention that spooks' location under the Official Secrets Act. Or anything else that might come up with it....I've probably gone too far already, you know?"

"Oh, I see. You think that, do you, that we could be monitored?"

"Truthfully… I don't see how they could be bothered. But…"

"We are in communication all the time, aren't we? I'm always hearing that it works both ways."

"The laugh is they know my story better than I do. … Here we are… almost on the doorstep."

"Thanks. It's much appreciated….. Did people laugh at you selling the 'It's All Lies' Socialist newspaper?"

"There I was in middle of Glasgow's Sauchiehall Street, London accent, shouting 'Get your Socialist Worker here!' Sure, they took the piss, I was trying to sell it to prove how committed I was, couldn't see the humour in it, till Jennifer came along and said, 'Can't be worth twenty pence then'."

"Thanks for letting me know something of the man I am sitting next to. Goodnight."

Recording transcript 4

"Good morning."

"Hope I'm not too late. Thanks for letting me meet you here. Well now, have I got something to tell you."

"Me first…I'm leaving her, that's it, after all the nice things I was saying about her yesterday. The ugly side showed itself up. She screamed at me. Her brother yelled at the top of his voice. 'David get control of yourself.' Funny isn't it? Using your full name as if that's going to change the situation. That's it, I'm off. Closing the books. Don't need that, that kind of treatment."

"Go on then, you first. What happened?"

"Excuse my language, but the fucking priest got his tuppence-worth in as well."

"I think you should start at the beginning, calm down, I can see your veins."

"Sorry…Okay. When I got home early yesterday. Well, you know that Tory, Malcolm Sutherland MP, the one I told you about, from our days in Scotland. He was just leaving in his car. I thought about him again. I once hoped he had forgotten her and we could live in peace. But not so, like a bad penny, from time to time over the last decades he's shown up. One of her 'gypsies' out of the blue. I was just about civil and he waved like he was dying to see me but had to rush. They were there, her brother and the Priest. I felt they were put out to see me.'You're early' was about all she could manage. I noticed how stiff she became as soon as I arrived.

I felt they all were. Finally she said 'Did you catch Malcolm? He was hoping to see you.' 'We were about to eat' she said, 'I suppose you would like to join us.' They already had opened a bottle. It was nearly empty, another empty one next to this Priest. Somehow I felt rubbed up, instead of going to my den. I decided to sit it out."

"Was you looking to be awkward?"

"I think I might have been. They made it worse. Instead of asking how I was, or, how's your day been. Even if they weren't interested they could have been polite. No, they went straight on talking about suicide, half-brother Toby claimed he had several times been near to taking the decision. I said that's the first I've heard of it. Jennifer said I was to be quiet. In my own bloody home, would you believe. Be quiet in my own home, I ask you! It got worse when she accused me of being bloody minded. Toby stood up, said that Father Ignatius Xavier had just told them, before I came in, that he had reached the end and was contemplating doing it.

And that's when he, Toby bollocks brain, shouted at me."

"What is there about this Priest, then?"

"Apparently he is from Rwanda - you know, funny things went on there. Hutus killing Tutsis or the other way round, whatever it was I asked which one he was."

"I saw the film. I couldn't take it. The kids and Maggie watched it to the end."

"It all went belly up when I said I would like to know in advance if someone living in my house was about to do something like that. It's only reasonable."

"Living?"

"Yes, for a week now. He's got the spare room; the twins are at uni."

"All I said was I hope he isn't going to do it here. What with me being in the Police and all that. Jennifer started to scream with laughter, not real laughter, mocking laughter, she became almost hysterical."

"I didn't think priests were allowed to do things like that."

"Especially in my house. They couldn't see it. They both said I was insensitive and that I always had been. I am the one going out to work and paying for it."

"I thought you said she earned money as a, what's it?"

"Counsellor."

"What was the Priest doing throughout all of this?"

"He helped himself to more wine then started sort of laughing as well. Toby said I was nothing but a plod, just like the ones who stand outside the scene of the crime, pretending they've got something to do with the investigation. 'As important as a piece of shit,' were his actual words.

"I was stunned, doing all this overtime, paying for the

kids," Jennifer said. For all she knew I was making up to you. They all laughed again.

"What? Why in hell's name would she think like that? What has given her the impression? Have you been claiming? What have you said that gave her that impression?"

"What started that was, I sort of joked that the Tory MP had probably come round sniffing his oats and that the Priest was praying that he could join in and have a threesome. And I poor muggins was paying for her sex life. She threw my mother's tea pot at me and they all left the room. I sat there all night on my own. That's it... I'm not going back, fuck 'em. I've taken a sleeping pill."

"Right then I will tell you what happened to me when you wake up."

"Oh and by the way, it's another short shift."

"What a cheek ... I hope you put her right about us."

"She didn't really mean it... I've told her you don't fancy me."

"The thought never entered my mind. Oh my Lord what a thought! I was going to say sweet dreams but I don't think I will now. Another short shift. It makes you wonder what they are up to. I'm sorry. Take it easy... relax."

Recording transcript five

"Here I am… awake and ready for in-action."

"I brought sandwiches today ……Do you want one? Bun and cheese."

"Thanks I will have it later. My mouth is dry. Anything to report?"

"Nothing I don't even think that he is here…Try this drink it's my favourite Sorrel, cos that's just what it is."

"That does refresh."

"There was this woman looking in cars…She looked at this one. I pretended to be asleep."

"What? What did she look like?"

"It was raining then. She had an orange raincoat."

"Orange? No."

"I thought she was looking for someone she probably had promised to meet someone and was checking out the cars…..to see if she could find them."

"What a bloody fine detective you would make. That was probably Jennifer. I wouldn't put it past her. Checking us out."

"Well, knock me down. We are supposed to be undercover. And people are spying on us! Well, forgive me for being shocked. Fancy that - being checked out by someone's wife. If it was her… Curly hair?"

"Yes. I think I told her where we were. If it was her what did she want? Did you see if she looked in the cars behind us? She would have seen us both asleep then."

"I didn't see. I didn't think to. She was gone."

"It's time to take you home. What was it you were saving up to tell me?"

"Yesterday evening when you dropped me I turned the corner and I could see that all the lights in my flat were on. And there was a big car parked awkwardly in the forecourt. I felt something was up. You won't believe who was there."

'Who?"

"Tom, Dick and Harry I call them. The lads, all three of them, you know the ones who were waiting for me the other night. The children were up, my sister was actually getting them ice from the fridge, a bottle of Wray and Nephew on the table, all laughing their heads off. I shouted at them 'What the hell are you doing in my house?' Them say 'Don't worry Mother we are undercover police officers' and showed me their identification. 'Well, that's all very well,' I said, 'But who invited you in?' You won't believe this but my sister had done just that, she even let them in on my nicknames for them. The rude one I call Tom apologized for having said shut up to me the other night. And I was right about him; the African one, I called Harry, also apologized for being rude. So I said was the well spoken intelligent one's name Richard? 'No Dick' he said and with that they all started to fall about as if they were on something stronger than rum. The kids were loving it, so was Maggie. 'Well, what do you want?' I asked. 'Nothing' they all said, 'we just wanted to make it up to you'. And before you know it they sent Harry out to get some fried chicken and bits for us all. Tom and Dick took their shoes off and stretched out on the couch playing with my kids. I just stood there. It was a long time before I took my coat off. Later they explained they were targeted on the Roman Road. They didn't want to say too much but as I did surveillance, I would understand. They were allowed to have a bit of a free rein. I told them that's the last thing I have; actually I didn't want to understand, thanked them for apologizing and when they had eaten, would they mind moving on? Would you believe Maggie and the kids turned on me? They was enjoying the attention, so I asked straight out 'Who killed Auntie Yvonne then?' Dick said something about that being an interesting question, changed the subject as quick as a flash, they all left."

"Tom, Dick and Harry, eh? Were they scary? You know, hard men?"

"I expect that they could be. Although I must say they didn't feel like a threat. Two of them had what I call 'innit' accents, talking and sounding what's nowadays called street, and although they did it well, I could tell it wasn't of real Caribbean origin. When Dick spoke sometimes I could detect what you would call an educated voice. I liked him the best. Still I was furious with Maggie letting them in and we had another row. This time she complained that I was so stiff and never let anyone into my life. If I didn't change my attitude the kids would suffer. I had never kept a man long enough blah bloody blah. I screamed at her and went into my room and tried to fathom out what it was that the three undercover detectives were up to. How did they know what time I was coming home? Were the local police giving out my details? Are we now under surveillance? Had I seen something at the funeral? Should I go further into this? Should I seek advice, and if so, from whom? You know, Dave, I try not involve myself in local matters."

"But now it's out …and you will have to live with it…I want you to take the car home tonight, I'm …well… going to stay in a motel. Okay, I'll get out here. Drive carefully."

"Dave wait, I've been thinking. I mean are you doing the right thing? You and your wife have after all been together for a long, long time. Longer than most people I know. Look I hope you don't mind me putting my bit in but…"

"Well, I don't think it is your business. But thank you for being interested. I got to work out where I am in it all."

"It might have been her, Jennifer, she might have borrowed an orange coat and…"

"It probably was and I want to show her that I'm not an appendage. I have feelings and…"

"Are you jealous? Do you think you might be? You know she surrounds herself with these interesting people?"

"And I spend my day with you?"

"Well?"

"For all I know she might actually be jealous of you."

"What, living in a tower block in tubeless Hackney? Amidst hopeless youth unemployment and a Council that's sold off all the youth clubs? Where not so long ago Nigerian Town Hall teams were handing out the good properties to their own for bribes. Murder miles, knives. Not to forget the invasion of the Yuppies who in front of our eyes ethnic cleansed the best bits - gated homes and CCTV. And don't get me started on how they poshed up Broadway market."

"I think from what she said last night, she might, she probably is, jealous of us."

"What about, getting overweight, trailing people we hardly know anything about and with no means of doing anything about anything if anything happened? Forget it."

"She knows we talk… Jennifer and I were once closer than we are now. Told each other everything. Now we don't even talk. I don't tell her much and I don't listen to her chatter, as soon as I say anything that's it, she begins to turn her back. Then all of a sudden, bingo, she's down sussing us out. Fearful that I've got something she hasn't got."

"Well, I'm flattered."

"Shouldn't be if I were you."

"Good night."

Recording transcript six

"Where the fuck have you been?"

"You won't believe this."

"Try me."

"I parked the car behind the Hackney Empire, on a single yellow line way after 6.30 pm. I didn't want to drive up to the flats, so I would walk the rest of the way. There was nothing on in the theatre. And the, excuse me, liberty-taking bastards took it away at 10.30 pm. I've seen them prowling around looking for their victims, but I never thought they would snatch a car parked in an empty street on what everywhere else would be considered okay. On a single yellow line in an empty street after 6.30! It took me some time to trace it down and they wanted £250 to give it back to me."

"You told them who you are? Showed them proof?"

"I went further than that, I told them that they had interfered with Police surveillance and I would report them."

"I bet that made a lot of difference."

"I said why did they do this? Hackney Council had invested in the large vehicle removal truck so they were forced to meet targets. They claimed as the theatre was next to the Town Hall it was agreed they could target visiting cars when they needed to make up the numbers 'But is that legal?' I asked, and they laughed."

"You didn't pay did you?"

"No. But it took a long time, they had to check with our controllers and that took a really long time."

"That's bad news."

"Why?"

"It's not in our interest to draw to much official attention to ourselves. Besides we are now late going on duty. All of this will be noted and processed. Last night I stayed in a station house and there was a lot of talk of cutbacks and whatever it is we are up to is hardly front line. I was shown an internal document that didn't bode well for the likes of us."

"Well, I'm sorry, I just didn't want to draw attention to myself locally. Which incidentally proved to be a false hope. The word seems to have got out that I am a serving officer in the Met. There was a note waiting for me from the Muslim family downstairs asking for me to have a word with their son about mixing with the local gang, like I was going to traipse around the estate handing out words of wisdom. What do they think the Police are for? And my sister says that people ask her why there hasn't been anything about Auntie Yvonne's death in the Hackney Gazette and why hadn't there been an inquest. All of which has got nothing to do with me. I'm not even a proper detective and nobody tells me anything. I am, let's face it, an overweight lightweight…Anyway…So…How was your first night on the run?"

"Frankly it was uncomfortable, in more ways than one."

"Go on, spill the beans."

"Well, it was a dormitory. When I got there it was almost empty, but by the end of the evening was packed with out-of-towners up to take on a climate change rally. The laugh was that so many protestors' coaches had been used they had made the environment worse than if they had stayed at home."

"Did you meet anyone you knew?"

"Well, yes unfortunately I did, but …I'm not sure I want to tell. You know it's from my past and…"

"Okay, forget it. I need to relax, I'll do the Daily Mirror word puzzle then the crossword and…"

"After we left Bristol and before we went to Acton, we were moved into Walthamstow where I was ordered to become a foot soldier in the National Front."

"What, the British National Party?"

"No the NF. Different initials, similar thing. It was before the BNP."

"You've been about haven't you? Now you tell me you've even been with the racists."

"That's the job isn't it? It might surprise you to know that when they told me about you, they asked did I mind. With you being a black woman and all that."

"Who did? Well, I'm not surprised. Go on."

"Let's say the powers that be. It's ingrained in the Police culture. In recent years as I am sure you are aware it's been put on a top shelf of a Scotland Yard cupboard and identified as institutional racism. I don't suffer from it."

"I do though."

"Not with me."

"Oh thanks."

"Anyway, you're safe with me."

"Deary me, well carry on, before you get worse."

"It's nothing much to tell. It was so easy to join. Anyone could have done it. That is if you're white, of course. And then British."

"Surprise, surprise. I don't know why they don't let West Indians in. They're often as bad as the whites when it comes to the Asians. Nowadays they both all go on about the Poles … they don't seem to get the irony. In fact its alright not to like anyone from Eastern Europe around where I live."

"Who are often themselves more racist than local whites... Anyway I got recognised when my picture was printed in the Guardian and other papers."

"No!"

"I was in an Honour Guard, a scratch one that had been made up to greet an American white supremacist. He had sneaked into the country and the press had got wind of it. One of their lot told the leaders that I was an undercover officer. The National Front blew up the story, saying that the Police had known this guy was coming all along and the proof was that they had sent me to guard him. The shit hit the fan. It was hard for the top brass to say anything, so they just withdrew me."

"How did they know?"

"Well, I suppose it could have been when I was with the socialists, They made it their duty to confront the NF. There were lots of street fights and the fascists had people taking photos and that's probably where they clocked me. Of course it could have been an inside job. One of our own. Scary isn't it? After all there are a lot of fellow travellers in the Force. Jennifer hated that assignment. I had to stay away from home and cut my hair short. Like playing a part in a film, you know playing the bad guy and trying to look like you believed it. Method acting they call it on the training course."

"Did you do the salute?"

"Oh shut up."

"You did it? I bet you did. What was it like being in the master race?"

"Well, I didn't have to read books as I did when I was with the lefties. They are ordered to make a big effort to pretend they're normal, it's full of nutters trying to look normal. The most scary ones are the ones who actually read their narrow-minded literature. They don't look like the main lot, they dress in sort of quirky old-fashioned clothes and stand apart from the mob, considered themselves a cut above the others. Long leather overcoats and black Trilby hats. You can't imagine it. How hard it was to act so simple. The worse bit of all was spending time with the thick ones, who enjoy real crap things like getting their kicks sitting on a bus aggressively staring out immigrants. Luckily it didn't last too long. I feared I would have to get tattooed to prove I was in it. The controllers wanted me to hang out with the leaders, I avoided that saying that I was under suspicion, which it turned out I was."

"So what do they want apart from the obvious?"

"I don't think they know. Some do really hate everyone. Others take against those that don't look like themselves, yet eat curries and listen to all kinds of music and even cheer when a black guy scores a goal for England. Others have only got this one idea that is to hate foreigners and not allow any racial intrusion. Their latest pet hate, of course, is the Islamic lot. Yet they might have themselves a foreign sounding name or not know who or where their father was from, and they are really doing it to give themselves confidence. They like to feel they themselves actually belong here. They think they are the true inhabitants. They are in fact seeking identity I suppose you might say. A lot of them feel that they have been left out of what's happening generally in the world, they are noticing that they've been sidelined. As far as I'm concerned they're all a bit thick, blame the wrong people for the state the country is in and all that. But then there are the thugs, the real thugs, who are given legitimacy to hurt people and although the NF and the BNP nowadays pretend that they don't sanction it, of course they actually encourage it. They foster breakaway groups to do the dirty work, the English Defence League is the latest. How else do they get power but by creating fear? The socialists say that support for change would come from the workers in the factories or wherever people work nowadays. The tactic for fascists is to strive for power over the streets. Then they could say who it is that can walk down a street and who it is that can't. Some are real Nazis and other are narrow-minded patriots. I think it was Churchill who said we were a mongrel race. And the BNP say they love him. The thing is it's too late for them. That's what makes it so dangerous. they fester in a mixed society. Whether they like it or not they are in the public mind identified with violence. I believe that the real problem thing is they're not building factories any more. The real jobs are few and far between."

"This is where I come from whether they like it or not."

"That's what I know. It did me in. When you're undercover you have to will yourself to believe in whatever cause you've infiltrated. Otherwise you feel that you might let some doubt show on your face. You know, when you lie, you have to stare in someone's eyes and you force yourself to believe in the lie. You know what I mean don't you?"

"Look in my eyes and I will tell you that I have never lied. Policemen are supposed to be able to detect if the suspect is lying or not."

"That's the theory. Some people can do it. If you ask a searching question often people give their game away, especially if they think you know something already."

"So, were you asked was you a racist and hate black people and Asians and so on?"

"No. Strange at it might seem I wasn't asked that directly."

"You look the part, white on the thick side, definitely unlucky in love and carrying a grudge."

"You got it, especially around that time. As it happens I wasn't feeling loved and that helped me snarl when required."

"Was there anyone you could identify with? You know get on with?"

"Well, to tell you the truth I worked so hard at the part, I began to react and even think like them. So much so that when I met people who weren't really suitable candidates and had just got swept along on their coat tails I blanked them. I went for the zealots to get the nod from them."

"'If you believed in the part you must have in some part hated me."

"Sometimes I hate everybody...including you."

"Because I'm black?"

"Are you now? You know there must be something wrong with me - I hadn't noticed."

"Come on. How come you now find it easy to be with me? Let me look in your eyes and see if you're lying. Oi, don't put your shades on. How can anyone believe you're sincere, how come you can switch on and switch off? Perhaps you can't, perhaps you can't believe yourself. Can you believe who you are when you wake up? You're looking away."

"Because you sound like my bloody wife and now I've got you on my case as well!"

"Okay, don't shout."

"Look I had a rough night. I had to sit up with the guys and pretend it had all been a good laugh. The bloke who recognised me and told all the others about my business is a complete, I can't say it."

"Go on say it."

"No I can't. Look those days have gone. I am now stuck in the fucking car with you, sometimes twelve hours at a time."

"Not recently."

"Alright eight hours at a time. I don't like it any more then you do. We talk and already I've said too much. Why don't you get on with your fucking word puzzle and leave it out?"

"Sorry, I've obviously pressed the wrong button."

"I'm sorry I lost my rag…There, look in my eyes…What do you see?"

"Blank…even sadness. But after what you told me I can't see nothing, nothing much at all, did you ever hurt anyone…when you was Nazi?"

"I wasn't a Nazi. And yes I did. I hurt myself mostly. I had to take it on, like I was saying. I had to work on my snarl and push my chest out and clench my fists and stare long stares. My relationship changed with Jennifer. I…"

"Sexually?"

"Well, now you're asking. Actually yes. I'm not going there for your prying mind. You see, these men and they are mainly men, young to middle age men who are often seriously frustrated…."

"Sexually?"

"Are you getting off on this or something? Frustrated, as working class blokes can get if they don't have value, if they're not important to anyone. The trick is to make them feel more important, they are told that they represent something. After all, all they have to do is be themselves but feeling…"

"Snarl and stare and push their chest out."

"It's not only that. They get belief and comradeship. It's like when you first join the Force and the talk is of team spirit. That's what began to eat at me. The only way I could do it, was to look and feel like I was one of them. As I say, the way to do it is to teach yourself that…that you are a working class hero, one that belongs to a tribe. The best tribe in the world. And the great success is that all you got to do is look the part. Be one of the gang and stir up a bit of shit now and again. The trouble for the leaders was the bad press that the lads generated. The old NF didn't mind the notoriety as much, I think they revelled in it. Nowadays the BNP have to pretend they're respectable, not even racist, just realist, you know save the country for ourselves. British jobs for British workers, even Labour say that now."

"Do you think Mr Crow says that?"

"I very much doubt it. His union is as mixed as the rest of London is. You see all sorts working on the railways. Even women like you."

"Well, did you hurt anyone?"

"Yes."

"Tell me about it."

"No."

"How do I know you don't think those things now?"

"You don't."

"I feel sorry for Jennifer."

"Everyone does...anyway, I've had enough now...do your crossword or something."

"OK...Here's one for you. Three letters, what was Hitler's wife's first name?"

"Eva."

"I thought you would know...only joking, I hope you don't think I'm prying into your life...It's just that..."

"You know I actually don't mind...it does me good, to get things out...they have been bottling inside , quite frankly I don't have any one to talk these days…In fact I appreciate it, I find I don't mind talking to you."

"That's alright then I don't mind either…friends?"

"Shake on it."

"Where are you going tonight?"

"I thought I'd better go home."

Recording transcript 7 (Phone call to Jennifer Thwaite's house)

"Hallo, is Dave - David - there?"

"Who is this?"

"Um…. It's his partner. Pat…Patricia. DC Patricia Murray. I work with him."

"Oh, it's you is it? Listen I don't know what you think you're game is but then let me put it to you this way. I've heard too much about you already. So before you say anything more let me say this."

"Well, I…Is this Jennifer? I…"

"Yes. Are you going to listen? I don't know what you think your game is. But I must say that David is behaving most irrationally since he met you. He has starting shouting and verbally abusing me. A normally polite peaceful man is behaving in a most uncharacteristic manner. We like to live a quiet life, without anything getting between us. Do you realize he had a nervous breakdown a few years back? That he was on sick leave for almost a year? When he finally got this new assignment I felt relieved, he seemed to settle in. Now that he's got you as a partner his mood has changed. Hardly says a thing when he's at home. Shuts up like a clam if anyone asks him anything. If one asks him why, no rational answers are forthcoming. As I say he starts shouting when he does attempt to communicate. He is becoming increasingly irritable, locks himself in his room. You know he was wounded when he was in the armed forces? I bet he didn't tell you that. No, he wouldn't, perhaps he did. Who knows? Nowadays it seems he spends his time talking to you, about whatever it is you and he talk about. I for one am not happy about this situation. I hope it's not me or any of my business. Listen - are you listening?"

"Yes I..."

"Good because I don't want to have to tell you again. David is a very fragile man. And, and I don't know whether he's told you this but we love each other and we don't like secrecy and people interfering in our lives. So I suggest you leave him alone and ask for a transfer. He's not your type, not your type at all. So kindly desist. I don't appreciate you calling him at home. Spending all day with him is bad enough. A man like David rarely flips but when they do they don't need the type of distraction you offer. So what's the nature of your call? Will I have to write it down? Go on. Be brief. It's getting late he hasn't come yet, although I am expecting him soon. Well?"

"Please tell him that I won't be in tomorrow. My sister has been kidnapped. He has my numbers."

2. Internal Met restricted discussion document

Dear Superintendent Smyth,

Current Class 5 Surveillance Policy

Re.: Your request for a considered opinion on current Class 5 surveillance practice (238/11)

I must make my position clear. I have always considered them to be, quite frankly, surplus to requirements. They are an expensive item that is ineffective as a surveillance tool. The history of Class 5 can be traced back to the requirement of the Home Office and Government policy to persist with surveillance after a review by the cross-party Standing Parliamentary Police Committee. You will recall that questions were asked in the House of Commons of the Home Secretary and the then PM Tony Blair whether the full range of surveillance was still provided after the internal 9/11 review. That was in response to Opposition demands that the current practice be maintained and that political and other ongoing (non-Islamic) parties remain within active and operational police interests. As a consequence reassurance was given that the practice remained an ongoing priority. In response to these demands a policy was formed that answered the need that a so-called stake-out vehicle would be present on a rota basis on high profile targets.

This would be done at reduced cost:

A. In cases where the target could be under theoretical threat and police presence act as a reassurance and a deterrent;

B. In cases where there is extra parliamentary political activity and high profile media interest is ongoing;

C. To enable the Met to state that surveillance is ongoing and remained independent of MI5 or MI6 activity on an 'economic basis.'

Class 5 has evolved from armed officers trained to intervene, equipped with the latest electronic gadgetry etc to the present day practice to staffing the vehicles with low grade officers whose main duty is to fill the rotas and be present at the designated sites. These officers are often as not trained to respond and are, in effect, token and serve little purpose. The cost of this ineffective practice is still quite considerable, particularly where it is most likely that other agencies continue surveillance. I suggest that representations be made to the cross-party Standing Police Committee that a review be considered. Members of this all-party committee could be invited to assess the effectiveness of Class 5 and a two-month closure plan be offered. In the light that the practice of visual presence is no longer 'a hot potato' I feel confident we can return the officers involved to another suitable position.

Yours respectfully Mark Logan London Surveillance Coordinator

Scotland Yard

Recording transcript 8 (D.X Phone recording of visit to Patricia Murray's house)

"Anyone in?"

"Hello….Who is it?...Who's there?'

"It's me, Dave. David."

"Oh. Hang on. I'll undo the chains…Come in."

"I thought I'd better come round and check you out. I heard about your problems. It's been two weeks and I hadn't heard from you."

"Did your wife tell you I rang?"

"I didn't go home for a week. I couldn't bring myself to. I heard about your problems on the grapevine. Is there any news?"

"Well, where do I start? It's been the most harrowing time of my life. I can't start to tell you what I've been through. I don't know where I got strength to carry on. If it hadn't been for my neighbours Mrs Patel and the Constantine family upstairs and the need to protect my children I think I would have done myself in."

"Is there any news?"

"Where do I start?"

"Have you had Police help? Are the kidnap boys, squad, involved?"

"You know she's back home?"

"No…..I didn't…yeah? In fact I know so little. I only found out this week. I would have come earlier. I didn't know what to do for the best. Maggie is back?"

"Yes she is asleep in the back room. She is very distressed and can hardly talk about it. She is on medication. We have to keep our voices down. When she wakes I hear her crying. It's all too much…How about you, are you alright?"

"Never mind about me…Can you tell me anything? It might help to tell. If it's any use to you. It could help… Maybe?"

"I'll make a pot of tea."

"So, go on then, what happened? She's safe?"

"Yes and almost in one piece. They thought it was me they snatched would you believe. They took her to another part of London. And wait for it … actually you won't believe it. They put a bag over her head as soon they got her in the car."

"They thought they had you? How did they get her in the first place?"

"Quite simple really, a nice spoken white man, middle aged, looked official, knocked on the door and said he had come urgently to take her to her sister. Her to me, I mean me to her. They thought she was me and they took her thinking she was me."

"To meet who?"

"He even waited until she took the kids upstairs to the

neighbours, so convinced was Maggie that she thought it was legitimate."

"Mistaken identity? That sounds pretty dumb of them. What did they want from you, do you know? When did they let her go? Why did they want you in the first place? Who are they? Who is it that wants to talk to you? How was Maggie freed? Do you know the answers?"

"Well, I'm not sure about everything. Maggie took them seriously. I suppose seeing her with the children they thought they had me. She said that the man said 'Mrs. Murray?' And she actually replied 'No it's Miss.' Anyway when I got home I thought there was something wrong as the kids were still upstairs with the Constantines. It wasn't till later that I listen to the phone messages and there it was. This time it was a black voice. 'We have your sister and if you co-operate nothing will happen to her and don't think of calling the Police or something unfortunate will happen.' It was then that I rang you…I gave it to the next morning and that's when I called in and reported the matter. They sent round two very professional officers who quickly came to the conclusion that they had snatched the wrong person and that it was entirely possible that this wasn't your usual kidnap. While they were actually interviewing me for the umpteenth time, there was another phone call saying it was a mistake and that as soon as the coast was clear they would let her go. As they were watching the flat and had seen that I had called in the law, this would delay her release. They said there was nothing to worry about. Imagine that! That they wanted to talk to me that was all. They would tell Maggie what it was about. The last man apologized for the inconvenience. Well, the officers traced the calls, one was from Brighton and the other was from Walthamstow. After a while the kidnap team seemed to lose interest; that's how it looked to me. They said there were lots of kidnappings going on so they were being sent elsewhere. As this wasn't your usual case they would have to monitor it differently. They would wait to see what would happen next and as my phone was now tapped I should relax. Imagine that! They would have the local CCTV looked at. It was like they weren't that concerned. As I was a serving officer they needed to check me out. Check me out would you believe? They kept asking me what I thought it could be. It seemed that they were convinced it was work related. At the time I couldn't put two and two together."

Like our Bob Crow work had something to do with it... what a laugh ...for my part I haven't got a clue what they could be talking about."

"It was to do with Auntie Yvonne. Maggie told me. She didn't tell the officers that when they brought her back...She just cried. I think they decided it was all a big mistake and left saying they will keep the case open, especially as I was a serving officer. I felt that they were thinking they had more important things to do. They acted as if they had solved the crime."

"Auntie Yvonne again - what is it about her? Are you sure you don't know what is?"

"She was always a mystery and I mean to find out what it is and why just going to her funeral seems to sparked off interest in me...The thing is ...Maggie didn't want publicity. She was sexually molested by some of her guards, which has freaked her out. Most of the time she wasn't blind-folded or tied up or anything like that, she was kept in a locked room though. It seems that some youths who were part of the scene took advantage of her not totally but…"

"What do you mean? They played about with her? I mean, forced themselves onto her sexually?"

"She doesn't want it to come out…locally. I've gone along with it…she is however talking to certain locals and she has apparently been threatening to go see some heavy duty boys who she knows who went to the same school. And ask them to take on her rude captors or guards or whatever game those certain lads was at. The ones who did the molesting."

"How would she know how to find them?"

"The thing is, it was Tom, Dick, and Harry who broke down the door and released her."

"What a story. There is so much more to this than I expected. Actually I didn't know what to expect… you've been away for two weeks. I was worried then I got the tip you had these problems…But that was put to me in a way that I shouldn't be too worried, you know. I'm sorry that I didn't make contact sooner."

"You know when you are in a situation and you aren't sure what it is, that's how I feel. Strange a policewoman who nobody rates, a dogs-body, has to become her own detective."

"Oh you think you should inform higher up about the Auntie Yvonne connection and those three cops?"

"Yes probably, but when I have worked it out for myself."

"Can I help you?"

"Yes I suppose it would help to have someone to tell it to. We will need to find the so- called Tom, Dick and Harry. You know the kidnappers apologised to her, sort of officially."

"Who did?"

"John Smith."

"John Smith? What John Smith?"

"John Smith, John Smith of the Smiths. You know the Smiths."

"What, the band?"

"No the criminals, the families, the heirs to the Krays none other than John 'the Badger' Smith."

"Oh, him – really? Him! He really is a villain. A sort of number one bad guy, almost the nation's official bad guy. Fuck. Now I know who you mean… It's funny isn't it, about the name 'John Smith.' For a moment I thought you were having me on. Like when Americans say John Doe. Actually we know the one who's being talked about. This guy is a very well known John Smith …indeed. And you've just got to believe him when he says who he is… if you know what I mean?"

"He apologised for what happened to her - he said to Maggie, 'It isn't what was meant to have happened. Here's five hundred quid, in fifty pound notes. without any reservations, sorry about the bag over the head.' He said he would cut them boys loose, who messed with her. 'I want to meet your sister Patricia ASAP. To talk about Auntie Yvonne's murder. That was it."

Recording transcript 9

"Tell me some more about her then...Auntie Yvonne?"

"Auntie Yvonne came from Jamaica around the late fifties, early sixties. She was either from Spanish Town or downtown Kingston, people aren't sure for certain. She was nobody's but just about everybody's aunt, if you know what I mean. She was everywhere - everywhere you went, she would be there. Earliest thing I ever heard about her, was that she helped my parents get a house. Remember this was way back in the day of 'No Dogs, No Blacks and No Irish'. People in them days, black people, would come together and help each other get started. One by one they would help each other to raise the money for a mortgage, until they all had a house of their own. That's how she became known as Auntie by many people. Helped them you know, one way or another. You would see her on top of a float at Carnival. 'Ooh, look, there's Auntie Yvonne!' your mum would say and make you wave back at her. I saw her sitting on a platform with Ken Livingstone when he was first ever running for Mayor. Another time she was in the Hackney Gazette with Prince Charles and another time behind a little girl presenting a bunch of flowers to Lady Diana. On election night she was on telly congratulating Diane Abbott when she became the first ever female black MP. She wouldn't have helped or anything with the campaigns, but there she was, as bold as brass in the spotlight. She was quite literally everywhere, every marriage, every christening and every funeral. People would say that you didn't have to send her an invitation cos she would be coming anyway. A 'thin, sinewy woman', she took big steps when she walked. She would turn her head right and left so that she could take in what was going down in the neighbourhood. And when she saw what it was she wanted to look at, she would screw up here nose and stare intensely through her big horn-rimmed glasses. It could be disconcerting. An old-fashioned type really. Big hats, straight hair and what folks used to call spinster clothes. Praying in St Anthony's Church with loud 'Hallelujahs' whenever she could, she was on every committee she could get onto but never turned up most of the time."

"Did she ever marry?"

"No."

"Who did she live with... anybody?"

"I didn't even know she had a sister till she actually rang me and told me about Auntie Yvonne's unfortunate end, some days after I had already found out. She had the same warm comforting Jamaican tone. But they hadn't seen each other for years. Not until Auntie Yvonne went home and soon after was killed."

"Where did she die? Not in Jamaica? In Jamaica? You didn't tell me that before. Isn't that why you don't know if there was an inquest? I mean, do you know anyone in Jamaica nowadays?"

"Well, yes we do. My mum and her sister sold up and went to live in Mandeville – that's a long way from Kingston. I doubt if it was in the local papers over there. I doubt if she was known over there at all. My mum hadn't heard when I called her last week."

"You said she was a grass over here. An informer?"

"A paid informer at that."

"How did people find out?"

"It became obvious. She didn't approve of crack for instance. She told me, when I was quite young, that she told the authorities on people who were being naughty. Some loose Yardies actually did time, it was put down to her, never proved though. The last thing I heard was that she led the drug squad to a house where some Vietnamese were growing skunk. She didn't need to tell them - the whole street could smell it. They were doing DVDs as well. It's strange isn't it, but my training to remember and note down facts is paying off at last? I spent most of the night assembling in my mind what I do know."

"What you haven't said was why she was sent back to be buried here."

"It was in her will and even the cost, apparently she had left almost the exact amount. It's funny isn't it? I went to the funeral in Kensal Green."

"You didn't say Kensal Green cemetery before."

"Anyway. I went there out of respect and now I'm up to my neck at it... I wonder – if I hadn't gone, would anyone be interested in me? That must be the case, mustn't it?"

"My auntie was also buried in Kensal Green."

"So what?"

"So nothing...what happens next?"

"I'm expecting a car in about an hour's time."

"Really...What shall I do?...I don't know."

"Well, nothing."

"I don't feel I can just let you do this. I feel that …"

"What you feel doesn't really count."

"Thanks...well. What kind of a bloke would I be if I didn't try to help? You're my partner for Christ's sake."

"The way I think is that what's my problem, has got nothing to do with what kind of a bloke you are. You know what I mean? Thank you for coming round, actually two weeks later than when I called you. No disrespect intended, but you emphasizing, 'Partner' right now doesn't help me much. I mean I've got a sister beside herself, shocked and spitting out revenge in between crying fits, threatening to confront the Smiths no less. And now I'm sitting here waiting for a car probably full of thugs, taking me to meet who knows what. I would probably prefer it if you went now...thank you for coming round."

"Let's Google John Smith."

"I already have."

"And?"

"The Smiths keep appearing for twenty pages, all of them, but especially John the Badger Smith. You learn that he's not called Badger cos he likes the furry creatures, or that he lives in a burrow and gets by eating ants. It's because he got his reputation for badgering people. There's so much stuff that he and his family are into. It's hard to find what he hasn't been accused of yet he's hardly ever convicted. His dad made money after the war, buying bombed-out houses. He was sent down for assault at the Old Bailey and was known as the Big Man of the Roman Road. He got ten years. Badger was the oldest, must now be into his seventies. While they don't get nailed very often, there are numerous tales of protection, drugs, pimping foreign girls, property swindles, jury tampering, even murder."

"All of which I imagine they deny."

"Did I say tobacco smuggling, firearms offences and currency laundering? One of the younger siblings, Freddie, is in jail for stealing cement mixers and taking them straight to the docks, putting them in containers and sending them to Jamaica where he was building a mansion. Probably still is."

"They help themselves, then."

"You could say that."

"You are being very brave then. Going to talk to them. I mean how about that? What has given you the confidence to do this?"

"Well, the way I got it figured, if you're really interested, is that the Smiths know I'm some sort of a police officer and that the Met's kidnap boys have been involved. That Maggie would have told us who they were anyway.

Don't forget they gave her cash they said with 'no reservations.' They must have calculated that as far as the Met was concerned, what happened with Maggie isn't important enough for them to move against them. Like, the fact they're currently on trial for tax evasion, as that's constantly on and off in the news. It was as good enough as said to me, almost officially, would you believe? That we were incidental…So, weirdly, I feel safe. Besides it's all to do with Auntie Yvonne. And you've got to admit that has become so big a deal that I would like to hear what they've got to say about it."

"If this was a film it would all be the other way round. I would be saying to the female lead not to follow me, and the audience would know she would and quite probably save him in the nick of time."

"Oh that's great to know that this is turning you on… Anyway it's not like that is it? The very last thing I want you to do is to have anything to do with what I'm doing in my own free time. In all seriousness shouldn't you be getting back to your Jennifer? Thank you for coming round."

Recording transcript 10

"Well, good morning."

"Hi."

"It's stopped raining and I think we are in for a nice day."

"That's good."

"Well?"

"Well…thanks for not following me."

"As if I would have."

"Thanks anyway for being interested etc…I'm sorry if I was a bit tetchy yesterday."

"Well?"

"Auntie Yvonne was murdered by Leroy the Flee Man Stuart."

"Really, so who's he?"

"He apparently is an illegal something or other, what's called a Yardie, brought here by the Met to work undercover, without legal status. I'm not sure of his status, but he was in the country to help with some of their investigations."

"Was?"

"They thought he was in hiding in Kingston or up in the Blue Mountains. Now they're worried that he could actually be back here. His nickname says it all: Flee Man. In other words he almost always gets away."

"Who told you this?"

"Who do you think? John the Badger Smith!"

"No less…What was he like?"

"As you might expect, a perfect gentleman, almost a cliché of one, he was waiting outside for me. Shortly after you left a charming young East European-type woman arrived, said she had a baby-minding certificate and was prepared to look after the kids while I was away. As if I would do that. Maggie was still under sedation. So I put them upstairs with the Constantine's."

So what is he like?"

"You wouldn't trust him as far as you can gob, but you do. Know what I mean? At one and the same time he is engaging but it's easy to see beyond that. He's obviously ruthless, gets his own way with everything and to hide that he pretends to let you make choices. 'Would you prefer to sit in the back?' he asks, having already opened the door and you think, where else am I going to sit, with the chauffeur? He was waiting for me in our forecourt, no less. As bold as brass, standing in the most obvious point of vision for the CCTV cameras to clock him, all done up like a celebrity, posh overcoat, treated hair, tanned. But not overdone, not your average Roman Road sun-lamp job. Money has bought him style. The car we got into was one of those Lexus good-for-the-environment numbers. 'Would you like to go to the newly opened Port Royal club on the Isle of Dogs?'

As if I had a choice. 'Maybe get a bite to eat, and we can talk things over. Are your children in good hands? We won't be too long I'm sure. I hope you agree, it would be helpful to be somewhere nice and relaxed so we can talk things over'. Those were his words, or something like that. Of course I agreed. About five times in the next two hours that it took us, he apologized for what happened to Maggie. 'Will she forget it after a while, she will won't she?' I managed to say while I was still in the car, 'I wouldn't have appreciated having a black bag put over my head and being molested by some yobs.' He looked put out at this and I felt for a twinge of a second that he was going to get cross with me. 'No,' he finally agreed, 'I can't imagine anyone liking that. My instructions were quite clear. To make sure that you were invited to meet me and to speedily arrange your journey here. My men can get it wrong, too enthusiastic to get the job done.' He said, 'I was mortified when I heard how your sister was treated,' and so on. His voice was a strange mix of your genuine Roman Road east end and as if he had had lessons. Sometimes when he spoke it was if he was listening to himself speaking the words, and checking that they sounded right. Anyway we got to the Port Royal, which turns out to be named after a part sunken city near Kingston, Jamaica. I though how typical he's brought me to a West Indian gaff. Type for type, eh? But, I must say it was very nice there, swish. I counted three types of curried goat; they even had jerk pork done in a clay pit, different shades of rice 'n' peas. I said I wasn't hungry although I was starving. We went in a small conference room and straight out he told me who killed Auntie Yvonne. And slowly he got around to asking me what my involvement in the matter was. Well, I couldn't make up my mind whether or not to be a bit cagey with him. Whether to tell him that I had come to the funeral because I had a phone call the night before and was informed that it was on. I just happened to be late otherwise I wouldn't have been noticed at all. I was as bold as I could be, when I said that it was my own business, and it should suffice to say that she was my Auntie and I had come to mourn her surprise death.

"Well, he could understand that, he said. He explained that when he had been told that I was a policewoman he was surprised, because he had already been in touch with various Met departments and they had told them what they knew, which he said hadn't included me. And he had wondered what I was doing on what was after all a Jamaican case. He said that was why he had sent for me. Again he was so sorry that his people had got the wrong message and had been out of order being rough with Maggie. He said he had been told by his contacts that I wasn't officially anything to do with any ongoing investigation. He pointed upwards and implied that there was surprise at the top in my involvement. The Flee Man had murdered two East European prostitutes while he had been in London. This certified killer had been a convicted psychopath in Jamaica and originally been brought over here to spy on a South London Yardie gang and it had all gone wrong. So eventually I asked, 'What's your interest? Did you know Auntie Yvonne?' Then I quickly asked before he was ready to answer the first question, "Do you actually know Leroy the Flee Man Stuart?"

"And did he?"

"He said that he had known Auntie Yvonne, she was a pillar of the community. And he had caught sight of the killer several times, once in this place and another at a dog track but never spoken to him. He said that guy had looked 'wonky', definitely deranged, had a reputation for not getting caught and being very dangerous and ruthless."

"And his interest in him?"

"He was worried for the girls."

"He is their pimp, in other words …Badger's Birds, as the press have it."

"I didn't say that to him. He waited patiently while I finished my drink. 'Now you know,' he formally stood up and clasped my hand, looked me straight in the eyes. 'Nice to have met you and sorry again about the stress my men caused you and your sister.' He would let me know about the pursuit of Auntie Yvonne's killer.'I promise that if I find out something of interest to you, I'll let you know.' He left, sent for the chauffeur to take me home. Just as I was leaving you'll never guess who I saw in the Port Royal Club."

"Tom, Dick and Harry."

"How did you guess?"

"Well, as you requested I didn't follow you but waited in the car outside and saw you leave. And then Tom,

Dick and Harry turned up and collected the pretty babysitter."

"Well, blow me down, I didn't let on that I had seen them."

Recording transcript 11

"Well?"

"But …How did you know they were Tom, Dick and Harry?"

"Well, wouldn't you like to know."

"Don't be irritating, of course I would like to know… Well?"

"At last I'm useful, so be polite. I will tell you some of what I know, by the end of the night, I think we will know a lot more. Let's hope that all will be exposed, as they say!"

"Polite? I'll punch you, hard, if you don't tell me… soon."

"I put two and two together. Three black guys out on the case, so to speak, and I asked around, used some of my contacts, you know, and bingo, it was obviously them. I was told that they were situated in the East End and were on a very loose rope indeed. Almost working for themselves was the way it was put to me. My main informant told me when I met up with him last night that they are to be found most nights at – guess where?"

"Where? I just can't guess… Oh, the Port Royal Club. The very one I was at last night."

"Exactimo… they're on 'excused boots'… an old army term meaning light duties."

"That was smart of you. You were right, it was them.

But you wouldn't expect them to be running chores for villains, would you? I wonder what they're up to. Do you know any more?"

"Only that we should park ourselves in the Port Royal Club car park tonight I'm told, if luck is with us, much of what our three friends are about will be revealed to us. It does have to be tonight. Only… if you can fix it your end I'm free tonight … as it happens."

"I should imagine that's most nights isn't it?"

"Well, no."

"Jenny and I have been talking and I've been going home and we have been talking things over and…"

"The Priest and the brother in law?"

"Well, if you must know."

"I'm not sure that I want to."

"Well, anyway they want you to come round for something to eat. Sometime…soon."

"You're kidding, aren't you? Don't you think I've got enough on my plate? What with a distraught sister, kids I don't see enough of and the extra self-inflicted duties involved in getting to the bottom of this Auntie Yvonne thing…and with all that, which I must add seems to me to be a lot more appropriate, than eating food round your house with your estranged middle class wife and a crazy priest and your unfriendly brother in law Toby…I can't see why Mr Big Badger Smith wanted to talk to me…just to tell me who killed Auntie Yvonne. And I don't believe for one moment that he wondered if I was leading an investigation of my own. I just can't fathom it out. Do Tom, Dick and Harry also think, them being the Police after all, that I am working on the case? Forget it. There is something else going on. But what?"

"I'll tell them it's a no then."

"Why would they want to talk to a semi-educated, east end, Roman Road black woman? Do they want to know how I make jerk chicken or something? Or perhaps they want to know how I feel about being cooped up all day in a car with man with a murky background. As it happens, I still haven't properly worked out what we are supposed to be doing all day watching out for Mr. Crow. No thanks. Please give my excuses, tell them I'm far too busy. I just know how out of place I would feel."

"Well, they're interested in your case and Jennifer who is a trained counsellor thought she might help."

"What does she think the problem is?"

"Well, I told about your Auntie Yvonne and your sister and the stress you are going through. She said perhaps she could help and..."

"No thanks. I will arrange with my family so that we can both stake out the Port Royal Club tonight."

****

"I'm beginning to wonder, as we are one of the few cars parked outside the premises, whether we have drawn attention to ourselves."

"Should we be in the car park, over there, in the far corner under the trees?"

"It's too late to move now, if it gets busier and we see your three friends, then we could drive round the block and enter then."

What shall we talk about then?"

"Anything."

"Alright. Have I told you that the priest Father Xavier and I have teamed up and are mates?"

"Bless my soul!"

"I don't think he could any longer. I'm not sure he believes in God any longer."

"What's his problem then?"

"He was in charge of a parish that had an orphanage, although he feared they weren't safe where they were situated. He was warned that sooner or later they should be moved or alternatively flee into the bush. He went instead to appeal to a Bishop for help and what he calls guidance. They wouldn't see him. He was so outraged that he wasn't getting any help from the church's authority. He staged a one-man demonstration outside the cathedral. Meanwhile the kids were butchered and raped. You know terrible racial things went on. The French and the West stood by and let it happened. Nobody in the wide world seemed interested in the fact that another Holocaust was taking place in Rwanda. For all their "never again" preaching. For his part, Father

Ignatius Xavier feels he failed miserably, he should have died with his charges."

"Or helped them to escape."

"But he didn't, he says he believed the higher authority would intervene. He has lost his faith. What makes it worse for him is that the Catholic Church has allowed some of the priests who took part in the killing fields back in the Church. They are being scattered around the world. Because, he says, the Church is short of priests."

"Which side was he on again?"

"He is a Hutu. It was his tribe members who killed maybe a million Tutsis."

"No wonder he's sick. I suppose it's good of Jennifer to take him in. It must be hard knowing that he suffered so much. What can you do about it? What with him going to top himself and all. How did you get to be friendly?"

"I took him to see Millwall."

"From one lost cause to another, then."

"There look – there they are."

'All three. Harry's on his mobile."

"He is the small one."

"That's Tom."

"And the tall one is…?"

'"Dick."

"I wonder who he's looking out for?"

"And here comes the answer."

"Two – no, three – official looking cars and one sporty Jag."

"Who do you think it's going to be, Bob Crow?"

"Look it's… it can't be… I was told I would be surprised. That one there looks like Prince Harry… Is it? It is isn't it? What the fuck… a whole team of them… giving high fives to your mates. They all look the same , dressed in rugby tops. How many were there travelling in that car?"

"They all seem to know each other…. I don't believe it's them. They could be doubles, couldn't they? But why?"

"Nobody is getting out of the other cars. They must be the security. The visitors are going into the Club."

"What's it all about, I wonder?"

"Drugs. What I heard was that your three mates score for them. You know your top people, toffs, like to slum a bit, instead of letting them loose, getting their pictures in the press, the powers that be fix it for them. Basically Tom, Dick and Harry are a police safety barrier, they look authentic and score for them. Pretend to be chummy Black dudes and all that, they have a certain caché… You know in these circumstances. It makes it all seem real."

"Well, blow me. What with Gangsters, Royals, police selling drugs. I feel a little bit like your Priest, disillusioned…I wonder if it's got anything to do with Auntie Yvonne. Take me home I do need a break…this is too much stress for me to take in."

3. Toby's tale

'Jennifer... I'm putting this on disk... I'm leaving for Australia ASAP... well, maybe. It might well be somewhere else...for what will become obvious. I can't be exact for security reasons. Look, all will become clear. Basically I have got on the wrong side of the top-end gangster Badger Smith. I can't put it any plainer than that. At any moment, probably tomorrow, some of his boys may, will, be sent round here to sort me out and frankly, having done my bit, I am going to make tracks. So before I go, I will tell you my tale and I will see you when the dust has settled... perhaps a year or even more. I am really sorry.

After we had the famous meal with David and his stressed-out partner PC Murray, and having listened intensely through the whole proceedings, and followed the plot throughout the evening. I decided to change tack. As you keep on pointing out to all and sundry, 'Toby is someone with time on his hands and doesn't know what to do with his sorry life.' Well, this time I took seriously your criticism that I never contribute until it's too late. I chose the last thing you would expect me to do, I decided to find out who killed this Auntie Yvonne character. Don't laugh. Yes, as simple as that. In truth, I never thought it would be as simple as anything. Anyway, despite my intense doubt-driven internal deliberations, I decided to take a chance. I would jump in at the deep end. Why not? The way I figured it, David and - what's her name? - Patricia wouldn't be able to do a lot more. So I, me, acting as a free agent and also totally unknown to the protagonists, could inveigle myself into the crime scene and thereby somehow have a shot at getting to the bottom of the mystery. Perhaps you remember I have always nourished an ambition to be an undercover journalist and this is exactly what they would do. I know, I know what you're thinking: how naïve.

I have borrowed £500 cash from your secret hiding place. I will repay you as soon as I earn again. I have always repaid you in the past. Okay, there was that time in Goa, but you said that I could get off that one if I kept schtum, about you know what, which you must admit I generally have. The rest of my adventure comes out of credit cards which have no link to you and will carry me overseas. So don't you fear, I will now spell out the details. In case it ever comes to court and I, god forbid, am not able to pass on my evidence; such as it is.

On my first evening I went to the Port Royal Club and ate at the restaurant as I was hungry. I had rather a lot to eat and drink, you wouldn't believe just how expensive it was. I quite cleverly gave a reasonable tip and took a risk, instead of leaving through the main door, I walked into the Club Members bit and settled at the bar... I saw my waiter give a nod to the barman and hey presto I was in. From the bar stool, where I drank some very pleasant margaritas I watched the whole proceedings. All types of rich and trendy people were in there. Some dressed up formally and then there were your sort of City types, trying to dress casual, you know the type, pressed jeans and thick vertical blue striped shirts without a tie.

Then I saw three guys who in fact turned out to be the very same, our Tom, Dick and Harry characters.

It took me some time to figure out how to get close to them. It dawned on me, that as it might be difficult to repeat the same entrance trick two nights running, I had better make contact that very night; besides, there were the arm and a leg prices.

What I did was a bit of a risk and had to concede some information to be able to make the contact. Some of the City types were drinking near to where the threesome were playing a very leisurely but loud game of Dominoes. I got talking to a City broker in the loo and casually as I could, went over to my new found friend in the bar. As soon as I felt that I looked like one of the team, I stood up and sauntered over to T D H and said 'Can anyone join in?' 'No thanks mate,' 'No way!' and, 'Are you a member?' were the three answers I got.

So, I did it. I said, 'I know Patricia Murray and thought you might help me score.'

Before I could say the next line which was going to be, 'She didn't know I was coming here,' they were surrounding me. It took a long time for them to believe my story, if they ever did. Basically I had to tell them the truth about my spurious connection to the plot. As the story slowly tallied they relaxed their hold on me and eventually started laughing amongst themselves at my middle-class gall. Please Jennifer don't tell Patricia as she might well be furious that I have linked her to drugs; what with racial stereotyping and all that. After a while the intelligent-looking one, who I think from Patricia's description is Dick, said predictably and in an officious tone, 'That was none of your business,' and that their only interest was that Patricia had been seen watching the Willesden funeral and they had wondered, like a lot of people, why she was there. Apparently when they found out she was in the police force they had also wondered if she was on duty and that as it turned out she wasn't anyway. Plus the fact that PC Murray knew the deceased meant they were no longer interested in her, apart from thoroughly liking her. Dick said he was surprised that Patricia hadn't told us that they had, all three of them, a family meal quite recently with her and her sister and kids. One of them obviously took a shine to her sister. Dick I think, said he had worried that 'Certain bad dudes had also poked their noses in.' So that's why they had been protective. Then as if a collective instinct hit them at once they turned to a man and faced me. Now quite hostile one of them suddenly said, 'What kind of a cunt are you, approaching us?' and, 'What gave you the idea that we were involved in drug dealing?'

Tom poked me quite hard with his fist. I could feel the others surrounding me. I repeated that I was only following a hunch as Patricia worked with David and I heard how you guys helped Maggie and that you also went to this club. They stopped me there and asked, 'How did Patricia know that we come here?' I had to say that she had seen them on the night that she met Mr Big. But Jennifer, be reassured, that's all I told them, as you will see in a roundabout way. It helped. At no time did I let on that I knew that they were undercover cops, although in fairness they must have worked out that I knew. Nor did I give the faintest hint that I knew who some of their clients were. I'll tell you what Dick was now, friendly arm round me, you know. 'You go and sit by the bar and have a few more drinks.' Which I did. They said they would see to me at the end of the evening.

I can't tell you what I went through, within myself, quite a paranoid time, pretending to be cool. I had risked a lot talking to them and had given a lot of my cover away. What did they mean 'see to me'? I was in truth shitting myself. Then a team of mixed-race minders came in with this older white couple and casually surrounded them as if protecting them. Later I realized that it was John Badger Smith and probably with his wife in tow. I got even more anxious. Well, I reasoned, nothing bad could happen if the proprietor of this gaff is actually in. Our three undercover cops enjoyed themselves, confidently they lounged around on the taxpayers' money, as if there was nothing going wrong in the world. Laughing amongst themselves, every now and again flirting with some beautiful passers-by. I thought about how plods like David and his partner spend their time in purgatorial stake outs. Well, at least your husband and partner are sitting down - better, I suppose, than standing on guard for hours outside the scene of a crime, pretending that they know what's going on inside when they don't know shit. Mind boggling and intensely boring it must be for them. And then, there are these guys. In comparison, same employer, living it up, with their fingers on the expenses sheet till, I'm sure.

One way or another I tailed them with my eyes. I never saw them once communicate with Smith and his prodigies. I was steadily getting a bit pissed by this time and despite how much it was costing me, us, I was determined to stick it out. I reasoned that as I had gone as far as this and would take what fate awaits me, so to speak there was no turning back. Well, I bet you're wondering by now, what in fact happened. It took me some time to figure out what in fact did happen. They actually gave me a Mickey Finn. You know, a drink or a smoke or whatever it is that sends you incapable. Knocks one out. As featured in all old-fashioned crime books and movies, I think you will find. Actually, it didn't quite KO me. This one sent me into a sort of semi-conscious comatose – I just sat outside the perimeter fence till late into the next morning.

At the end of the evening - I mean almost dawn - I was half cut already, when all three of them approached me and signalled that I should follow them outside. I remember that we went into the car park. I think the cold air hit me as I followed them around to the back of the club. The small one lit a big joint and almost immediately handed it to me. I don't know what it had in it but whatever it was it had a stunning effect. So much so that my legs gave way and I sunk to the ground. Like a bag of potatoes.

I sat propped at the back of the club for what must have been hours. I watched the staff close up and leave, some of them pointed to me and laughed at my paralytic state. Eventually I forced myself up and with great difficulty staggered out the main gate and there I slumped. I didn't feel the cold and luckily it wasn't raining. Jennifer, I just sat there completely zonked. Eventually these two guys came along and must have thought I was asleep. I could feel them looking in my pockets, and my satchel, which was just hanging around my neck, I thought they were trying to see what I had on me. By now I had some returning strength and I quickly stood up. You won't believe this but at the exact same time two Community Cops turned up, you know the ones who everybody laughs at, Blair's Boys in Blue, dressed like Air Force cadets. Anyway, they stood across the road from us and one asked if I was alright. The two suspected robbers actually stared at me and I could see that they were worried. I detected an almost pleading look in Wayne's eyes. They both moved away from me and then Winston made as if to catch me, were I to fall over again.

'He's had too much last night,' he shouted, all friendly like. One of the Community chaps took a picture. 'Just for the record.' 'What record?' said Wayne, and he started to cross the road but Winston whispered to him, 'Leave it out.' You could see that Wayne was a tough customer. 'They've got no right to do that,' and then quick as a flash he added, 'We are only helping a mate out. Something wrong with that nowadays is there?' I'm not sure why, but I went along with it. Wayne who I noticed was hobbling, turned back to me and said, 'They aren't allowed to do anything, they're a token, a joke.' I remember thinking, I'm not laughing. I reckoned that in more ways than one those guys were a blessing. I figured that as I have been seen officially in the company of these potential rascals, who at that time, I was sure, were intending to roll me but now they had second thoughts. I figured I was now probably safe, for a bit. Of course there were CCTV cameras all around. Although, they say, it's got to be serious crime for anyone to bother to look at them. Come to think of it I think it was David who told me that.

Anyway, when I looked closely at Wayne and Winston, I saw that both of them had recently taken a physical beating. In a desperate sort of way I could feel that both of them were now intent on being friendly with me. I broke the ice, 'Well, what happened to you guys?'

Jennifer, they both had swollen faces and bloodshot eyes, both limped and both had plaster round their right forearms. Winston managed a grin at the same time showing he had lost some teeth. 'We both got out of bed at the same time and bumped into each other,' he quipped. Wayne, who still had hold of my left arm, asked, 'Can you walk?' As I just about could, I found myself staggering along with them. We must have looked a strange trio. The token cops watched us until we turned the corner. 'What's your game bro'?' Winston asked. As soon as we were out of sight, I told them that I had been given a Mickey Finn.

'What in fuck's name is that?'

'I was drugged in such a way that I was incapable of movement.'

'What was it?'

'Some type of a cocktail, I think, and it took me up, down and sideways all at the same time.'

They both shrugged at each other and painfully laughed. Wayne asked me as he lent into my face, 'Was you trying to score anyway?' 'Well, yes,' I answered as earnestly as I could.

They both laughed again and said I should come along with them, which was a very slow process indeed. Eventually we reached quite a posh, flash Jeep-type car, which turned out to be their pride and joy. At first I was reluctant to get in. I made an excuse that I had to search for somewhere to stay, to live. 'No,' they insisted. 'Stay with us and we will find you a place as long as you got the readies to pay.' 'OK, I've got nothing better to do. And I can scrape together some rent.' I had hidden what was left of your £500 in my boots. 'That's cool, bro,' Wayne reassured me. And the 'bro' bit made me feel a bit safer. Well, for a while anyway.

I decided as we were cruising along, with a very loud sub woofer echoing off the surrounding buildings, that my new-found companions were a bona fide entrée into the sub-culture of criminal London. So I asked several times to make myself heard, 'Seeing you both have been so badly hurt, how come you left your vehicle so far away from where you met me, outside the Port Royal Club?' Both of them ignored the question. I soon found out why. I found myself in Hackney Wick, although it took me some time to find that out. The Wick, as it's affectionately known, is like a hidden land, once heavy industrial, now emptying as the nearby 2012 Olympic site takes hold. It's sort of a quaint place, a lost enclave, with extreme poverty and trendy artists who seem to get together in a cheek by jowl existence. It is situated in a corner of the Borough of Hackney, but clearly for a long time, until recently, quite ignored by it. A council I am informed, in recent years blew up the terrible tower blocks and built in their place some equally challenged new housing estates.

All this I learnt later, from a couple I met downstairs from where I stayed. What contrasts. In one building, budding artists whose dream is to enter the Turner Prize world, and on the next floor, desperate hoods and worse. Anyway, they took me to their flat on the second floor of this four-floor ex-Council type place. They seemed cagey as they unlocked the front door, taking a look round and about outside, then checking the inside before ushering me into a smelly and totally white room, replete with a blacked out window, a non-stop telly, two laptops and a distressed mattress on the floor. 'You can kip here and chuck into the kitty twenty-five quid a day,' said Wayne. 'Thirty-five', corrected Winston. 'Thirty,' I proffered. That's when I feared that there could be a nasty side to them both.

Winston advanced on me and poked my chest hard, as unbeknown to me Wayne had crouched down behind my back. 'T-H-I-R-T-Y,' he said, spelling out each letter, 'F-I-V-E fucking pounds,' as he pushed me backwards with his good arm. I hadn't anticipated the old trick – I fell over and banged my head on the telly. They both thought that this was tremendously funny even though it hurt them to laugh. Trying to get up I nearly knocked over the cardboard boxes carrying their expensive lap tops. At one and the same time both of them lurched forward to save their precious computers with their left arms, losing their balance they both fell on top of me whilst keeping in the air their precious machines. It turned out to be a magic moment, as laying in a heap of malfunctioning humans we couldn't help but to laugh, and laugh we did; the moment of malice had evaporated thank goodness. I was now thinking of making my excuses when Wayne said to Winston, 'We were only asked to get you off the street and now you are going to be a tenant.' 'By who?' I asked. After that doors opened and bits of the mystery slowly fell into place. It turns out that police Detectives Mendes, Onobolu and Flanagan - you got it, I bet: Tom, Dick and Harry - had virtually instructed my rescuers to come and pick me up and drop me somewhere central. Quickly getting over the fact that these two, as it turns out lifelong pals had actually hurt me by tipping me over, and how I was still overcoming the semi-sedated state I was in, I forgave them and now that we had genially laughed together and they for their part were now allowing each other to let me into their shared confidence. They are I soon realized great pals, into all sorts of shady business together and despite constantly challenging each other, they are a working team. Well, we drank their beers, then I paid for some quality coke and some real Thai weed that they happen to have with them. I bought some more beers they had stored and no change from a tenner. As the daylight dwindled we lit candles and talked way into the next morning. I heard and learnt lot.

The first thing you should know is that they were the ones who molested Patricia's sister Maggie, and that then they had worked for the Badger. They had traded their freedom with the cops by passing on information concerning the Smiths' business empire. They sell and can lay their hands on any drug known to man and significantly, some time back, they were on the roof when a local youth had been pushed off – an incident despite many others that is still talked of locally. They were at Auntie Yvonne's funeral and remember seeing the late arrival of Patricia and how locals described her as a copper.

Why, you might ask, were they being so frank with me? The answer is, I think, that there was nothing to lose. It turns out they recently realized their criminal careers had come to a dead end. I believe they felt better by getting it out of their systems - out, that is, with each other. I was an independent, the catalyst. I couldn't harm them and I believe I played a useful role. Which is, after all, a trick I learnt from you, my dear counsellor. As the evening wore on I let out bits of my reason for being there. They didn't seem to care. I would say that they were more interested in telling their tale than hearing mine. Between taking the piss out of each other, pointing up faults and remembering how wrong each had been in turn they got a lot off their chests. They were one moment laughing and then, moments later, getting angry with each other and then together slagging off third parties, friend and foe. I could see that they had travelled a long way together and I could see that they feared, although they never said as much, that they were at the end of the line.

The Police knew all about them and they now had a fearful enemy in the Smiths, who had them beaten up by the Kiwi twins, known as the Boxers. Apparently these two thugs don't actually beat you up directly but enjoy forcing you to fight them and if the victim at first declines they wait until you finally give in and one obliges by finally taking a swing at them, then they pummel you. If you didn't join in they warn that the guy lurking in the corner will throw acid over you for being a coward. They like to claim the injuries they inflict are 'In a fair fight'. I suppose that satisfies their antipodean sense of sport. Well, it seems they showed little mercy on Wayne and Winston who put up an energetic fight and got clobbered. At the end they were then forced to shake on it and the last thing they heard was "No problems, mates," before both of them collapsed. Apparently they were beaten up for their part in the Maggie business.

These guys had met each other in an orphanage of some sort. I believe it was in rural Wiltshire near to Swindon. Despite both being very bright, they had both spurned the opportunity of university in search of outlaw adventure. As our time together rolled on I began to see them in a different light. Underneath the hard show-off image, full of bravado and a seeming unconcern for anything that didn't communicate with them on their superficial wavelength, there were another two alter egos hiding beneath the surface. These guys had been successful at a higher education college both studying IT and video making. From what I gather they hadn't been rebels at the institution. It seems they had in fact integrated into the system. It was their success that eventually turned them off. They wanted out. They wanted to be living the life of wild bad guys. They would sneak off to London and imbibe in the hidden fruits. Bit by bit, I understood that they had rebuilt themselves and created an image based on the fashionable Jamaican swagger and gangster culture. As we talked this side of them gradually dropped away and they laughingly told me how at first they went over the top with the bling. 'Weighed down we were, like people robbing the temple.'

The big ambition was to hang with East End teams; with that went the danger that they could well outdo the locals with their derring-do. After a while Winston stood up to emphasize the point. 'You won't believe this. The local would-be hard men had mothers who kept tabs on them.' That isn't what you hear in the media is it, single parent mums cliché and all that? 'The local brothers had played at getting out of control and bragged they did some pretty wild things'. Winston scorned them: 'But they are being monitored by their mums who all went to school together and have power to rein local young people in and point a finger at those who go too far over the line.' 'That's how we met Auntie Yvonne,' revealed Wayne. 'She became our surrogate Mum, having a word with us when we went too far in the eyes of the Community.' As unaligned independents they found an easy living wholesaling drugs between the various factions growing up in Hackney and thereabouts. Then it seems along came the accelerating phenomena of young men shooting at each other and an abundance of guns to do it with. Some of the shootings were to do with the original rooftop incident and other territorial disputes and then it seemed for the sake of it. Africans against Caribbeans and the other way round etc., etc. The Murder Mile of guns and knives and silly kids making their "here today and gone and forgotten tomorrow" hard-man reputations. What had frightened them the most was the crack houses that sprung up and the unwanted involvement of hard-faced eastern Europeans and fierce territorial disputes between Tottenham's Turks and Kurds. So they found a way out. They went to work for the boss. They got a sort of contract to build a website for the Smiths charitable work, would you believe?

Winston put it this way: 'The Smiths are real professionals, they're in it for the long term and they're in it for the money, they can call on reinforcements whenever they want and they can afford to wait if they have to. They are sat plum in the middle playing off both sides and are into both horizontal and vertical integration. Wholesalers, manufacturers and retailers.' Then Wayne chipped in the inevitable, 'It was a case of, if you can't beat them join them, innit bro?' I wanted to ask them, there and then, to help me hunt down the Flee Man and to do that I figured I would need to meet with Mr John Badger Smith. Instead I asked them, in a casual sort of way, 'Do you know the Flee Man?' They both almost jumped out of their skins. Winston sprung up first, shaking off the effect of the stimulants: 'What, you've heard of The Flee Man, Leroy Stuart?'

Getting up onto his knees fast Winston asked his mate, 'Who the fuck is this guy?'

I tried to reassure them. 'I told you, I thought you were listening.' I said, 'Patricia Murray was personally told by John Badger Smith that the murderer of Auntie Yvonne had been done by none other than Leroy the Flee Man Stuart... I told you, about an hour ago.' 'You're fucking kidding us, aren't you?' They both seemed startled. I realized they hadn't been hearing my words; they had both been so intent on filling me in on their backgrounds that they had just ignored me.

I filled them in again and this time they listened. I told them I was your younger brother and that your husband David was a working plod whose partner had gone to Auntie Yvonne's funeral, that Tom, Dick and Harry had appeared and how the Badger had wanted to talk with Patricia and how they had snatched Maggie by mistake and how he told her that the killer was the Flee Man and how I thought that Dave and Patricia were unlikely to find the killer's whereabouts and that I have nothing better to do with my life and had decided to start my investigation by jumping in at the deep end. And here we all are.

There is I must admit a huge class and social division between the three of us. I felt I was coming across as a white middle class do-gooder and that if they hadn't been delegated by the three undercover policemen to move me from the Port Royal Club, we would have never met in a million years. Slowly they seemed to take it all in and I paid up for more beer and drugs and we relaxed again. I was anxious to ask about their film and video job with the Smiths. Instead of being drawn into my conversation, Winston let it out that Wayne had dated Maggie a number of times over the years and that they had set her up to be filmed in the room where she had been incarcerated.

They had given her some Es without her knowledge. She had relaxed when Wayne promised that he would take her home soon. They were ordered to wait a bit longer. They had got a bit familiar with each other and egged on by John Junior, Badger's oldest son, who instructed them 'they took it too far', which they reluctantly admitted. They had filmed the assault with a hidden camera and edited the tape to make it look like she went along with it. She was furious.

I asked, 'What was the point of the film?' The answer was that it was edited to look like she enjoyed being sexed up, and it could be used as a deterrent to stop her pursuing a case against the Smiths for her abduction.'That was pretty awful of you, especially as she was a friend,' I insisted. In truth both of them looked pretty shame-faced about it. 'And what's worse,' said Winston, 'the Smiths had changed their minds when the Police Detectives Onobolu, Mendes and Flanagan arrived to the rescue. John Junior had suddenly turned and blamed them, said it was the lads' idea all along.' 'In front of his dad he pointed the finger at us.' Hence their beating.

They both felt they had been saved from a worse fate, as the three undercover cops had advised the Smiths to let them loose. Instead, Wayne suggested, 'Let them became a handy target for the locals to avenge Maggie's distress. No one is afraid of those pussies, listen those bro's owe us, for fuck's sake!' It turns out that our three undercover heroes Mendes Onobolu and Flanagan, had originally got them into this flat. They had been told by DC Onobolu that if they wanted to remain protected, they should do his bidding. The deal then was for them to tell in some future good time, all they knew about the Smiths' business. 'As if he didn't know already,' is how Wayne noted it. They confided in me that they had now, despite the pressure, adopted a defensive and defiant attitude.

'Fuck 'em all!' Winston spoke for them both. 'The local wankers, the two-faced cops and the inbred Smiths!' 'As far as we are concerned, we know so much detail about them all, a lot of detail indeed.' 'And, we have it all on record, and that if we have to we will blow the whole thing up. Police and all.' Then looking me straight in the eye, suddenly changing subject, astonishingly he asked, 'What proof is there that the Flee Man had killed Auntie Yvonne?'

Wayne rose to the subject: 'She was close to the Smiths and the way they had turned on us proved that they were completely capable of ordering her death and blaming it on the Flee Man. 'How did he get back in the country?' 'It could have been any one of them who did it, she knew too much. She could have had the low down on any one of them and was about to grass them for all we know.' 'The difference between us and her,' claimed Winston, 'is while we can play along with the old Bill and the Smiths, they know that we have them all on tape and if anything happens to us, the whole world would soon find out what's what. She on the other hand was an old lady on her own.'

'Well!' I could point out, 'You came to collect me on the instructions of Tom, Dick and Harry.' They agreed but made it plain that they were giving the impression of playing along with the game. I could see it was their intention to get away as soon as they could. Winston spoke for them both when he asserted, 'We are well armed and if necessary we will shoot our way out.' Wayne put it succinctly, 'We've got nothing to lose and they all know that.'

You know, Jennifer, I believe them. As we spoke they got out their considerable armoury, from under the big cardboard box, an automatic pistol and a sawn-off shot gun. I was at first a bit frightened. They for their part behaved as if it was normal to do all this with their left hands and with some difficulty started to oil the weapons and load them. They didn't behave like kids with dangerous toys, you know, but like soldiers with quiet determination. I believe that they would reluctantly use them if they had to, and then would do so without hesitation.

Do you know, I think they had come to like me enough to tell and show me all this? I felt again I was a witness who had been let into their secret world. Having shown their cards, they told me a lot more, most of what I needed to know if I was to follow up my investigations. I felt it was time to ask, 'What are the Smiths into?' 'What aren't they into?' came the inevitable answer. 'Class 'A' drugs?' I asked. 'Nowadays they deal with both the endlessly warring Kurds and Turks and act as wholesalers to the rest of the country,' Wayne revealed and was open for more questions. 'Prostitution?' 'They mainly own the houses.' 'Protection?' 'That's how they got started. Some customers actually request it I believe.'

Jennifer, they seemed to suddenly shake off the inebriation, which had been ongoing for some hours by then. They both became amazingly articulate as both rose to the subject. I responded to it by paying attention by playing a role that I was only showing an academic interest in my best nonchalant manner.

It was yet to be some time before I could collapse with a head swimming full of tales of years of organized crime. It wasn't till two days later that I was able to try and remember a lot of what they had said during that intense session. I'm not sure if they wanted to get it off their chests or hear themselves list what they both knew or take advantage of a third party to bounce off - probably a mixture of all three. To an outsider it would have looked weird. The three of us sitting upright, despite wounds in a harshly lit room, guns and all, listening to a litany of nefarious wrong doing in a dispassionate manner as if it was the only time ever that this could happen. A truly unique moment for me. Winston correcting Wayne. The Smiths started after World War Two buying up bomb sites, selling black market contraband and getting into all the scams that were going. Long before we were born and on the scene. One of the old timers told me how they even had a business making dodgy sausages and selling them outside factories in the days of rationing and shortage. They made them from pink breadcrumbs that just shrivelled up when you cooked them. They love to boast about the past scams, as if reliving the good old days. It was all a great laugh to them as they robbed the mugs and got rich on the back of them. It must have been easy pickings as the country crawled out of postwar poverty and the Smiths could cheat and prosper and keep the cash hidden and, like the Krays, become respected in their own neighbourhoods. Winston said he heard that the Smiths would see someone beginning to prosper with say a chip shop and they would beat them up and take their hard-earned money and the victim or their family would never go the Police, who were frightened anyway. It gives another meaning to the word "respect".

Wayne had heard that one team just specialized in taking the lead off church roofs and another robbing pubs of their stock. It seems as they mixed in the Smiths' world they were treated to stories of legendry successes in crime, be it armed robbery to fraud, to stealing warehouses full of clothes, to physically sorting out rivals. They would tell the boys of the black-market goods stolen from the docks and the airports and sold in the factories; they would proudly claim that they could get hold of anything, any item they were asked to get, off the back of the proverbial lorry. It seems odd that these eager apprentices weren't to learn the ways of the criminals but only to listen to their boasting. For things had certainly changed as drugs entered the scene and globalization changed the landscape. I asked them straight out: what in their opinion was the core of the Smiths business these days? And they both answered without hesitation. 'Money laundering.' Winston described how in his opinion Badger had developed the banking side of the business. He said, 'All the dosh has to go somewhere. All the tentacles feed in their percentages and it can't all fit under the mattress. So they move it around for their clients and take a large slice. They okay activities, protect projects from competition and sort out those who try to sneak off.' They mix with all sorts. They don't like racists. Badger told me himself that there is no percentage in that. He said that he agreed with Tony Blair that we should open up shopping mall markets and do deals with like-minded organizations worldwide. Wayne confided, 'That's why they took us in. They knew we were connected, had dealt with both East End gangs of Tottenham and Hackney and with Kurds and Turks, Vietnamese and old school white Roman Road hoods.'

It seems that it was their IT skills that endeared them to the Smith mob. Badger, having taken advantage of Mrs Thatcher selling off the council housing stock, started buying up the numerous failed mortgages that had come steadily onto the market. There was a small fortune to be made from housing benefit rents and it was this respectable arm that apparently led Badger to consider a PR offensive and to Wayne and Winston learning video skills to make a film showing off Badger's good side, would you believe? Apparently, he likes to give to charity. Yes. The lads even filmed him dressed as Father Christmas at Walthamstow Market giving presents to dossers. They accompanied him to foreign climes. Having a well dug here and a water pump there. He met local bigwigs and posed for pictures. Much to his chagrin, the PR pictures never seemed to get published. The lads said that there were showings of the tapes mainly to in-house audiences. They got close to the family shooting and editing videos of family events, weddings, funerals, christenings, cars, paddocks full of horses, holidays, winter skiing, you name it, they were there and trusted. I suppose Badger's thinking was that he could have them nicked for all the untoward things they had done, or removed in a more sinister way if he need to. They played along, feeling immune they dealt with the various gangs, frolicked in all that was on offer. They made a tape of Auntie Yvonne's funeral and Winston reckoned that they even got Patricia in the frame. Badger had quickly taken the tape away from them as soon as they got back to base. That's the place where Maggie was taken, in Palmers Green.

They reckoned that Badger saw himself as a modern businessman. If he could have afforded to let go of his nefarious enterprise he would have done - gone legit. They reckon that the Smiths relied on their criminal activities as a bank. It financed them and their legitimate enterprises, some of which went belly up. Mrs Smith opened a health clinic down on the South Coast and it lost a fortune. A Gentleman's club in Hoxton burnt down and the insurance company wouldn't pay. Apparently Badger was so incensed that he threatened to take them out but he couldn't find anyone to finger. Rumour has it he set fire to their Holborn office in revenge. The Smiths lost loads of money in the recent City crash. Lots of their shares they had invested in tumbled. I had to laugh they way Winston and Wayne described it. Apparently Badger took it all personally. He would storm into the office with a copy of the Financial Times shouting out names of companies turning them into curse words. Fucking Woolworths and Northern fucking Rock. Even said that if he could get hold the fucking Icelandic Eskimos he'd stick the North Pole up their fucking polar bear arses. Badger said the Bankers had betrayed the nation and that Gordon Brown should shoot the fucking lot of them. That the one-eyed cunt missed the trick and poor investors like him were being ripped off because of it.

Wayne said that one couldn't laugh at these tirades. So they would shuffle from one foot to another trying to agree. That it was a shame, the way things were going. The sheer scale of the rip off! And the fact there was no way to punish the culprits. They both described Badger as almost taking off into space when he heard that the City folk were getting fat bonuses anyway. For a moment Wayne said, 'I thought he was going to make an alphabetic list of Bankers and one by one seek them out and have their fingers chopped off, but there were too many of them.'

And as Winston put it, 'he was a crap businessman but at least he had the crime to fall back on.' Shaking his head, Smith had apparently observed, 'At least I'm not one of those honest suckers.' I suppose you could say that's the way it's always been. Isn't that what the ruling class do when they come unstuck - go back to their methods of extortion, screw the peasants, while a robber baron like Smith robs the poor? It was about then that I came up with the idea that I could pose as a journalist and attempt to interview Badger. But first I must describe to you the rest of the week in Hackney Wick. Things changed between us when I accidentally fired the gun. What happened was this. We were laughing at Badger getting hold of the Chairman of the Royal Bank of Scotland and kneecapping him. I picked up the pistol and although I pointed it away from the other two, Winston remonstrated with me saying you should never point a pistol, which I hadn't, as it might be loaded. He pushed my arm upwards with his weak right arm. I went along with it. Inadvertently I squeezed the trigger. It was loaded and it went off. A bullet hit the wall. The bang was so loud if deafened us. Wayne and Winston started swearing at me. I couldn't hear them for the ringing in my ears. It would be an understatement to say that they were furious with me. Both got up, picked up their belongings, snatched the pistol out of my hands and calling me a cunt, over and over, which they built into a harmonic crescendo and screaming with drug fuelled laughter they suddenly left. I have never seen them since.

After a few minutes, into the room came one hesitant Ishmael followed by his tiny brothers and sisters. Obviously roused by the gunshot, timidly rubbing sleep from their eyes, looking quite frightened they stayed by the door. They had been asleep in one of the adjacent bedrooms but now roused by the commotion were daring to take look into the room where the reverberating shot had come from. Ishmael, who I formally introduced myself to the following morning, ushered his siblings back after satisfying himself there wasn't an immediate threat, gently closed the door behind him.

I started to write my notes. Finally I got to sleep in a room full of competing smells. The weed, the fags, the booze and the cordite mixed with the smell of eastern cooking that entered the room with the startled family. Jennifer, I was starving but I needed sleep more.

Day Two

I'll call it day two as I was in danger of losing my time bearings. Oh, and I had found out during the previous chaotic night's banter, that Badger owned the whole building that I was staying in. And what's more Wayne and Winston reckoned that the Flee Man had or even still has, when in London, a top floor apartment. I woke in the middle of the afternoon. Ishmael, I think it was him, had left a cup of an unfamiliar kind of tea beside my mattress, but it was now cold. I thankfully noticed that the lads had left me some keys and finding myself fit to stand up, decided to do something about my hunger. I had a very full English breakfast near to the big Tesco's in Morning Lane and got a bus to Tottenham Court Road where I bought this laptop with my credit card. I could have come home, sneaked in and got my own machine and quite probably bumped into you. As I would have had to explain myself I can just imagine what you would have said and, quite frankly, I couldn't have faced the inevitable criticism.

It was late when I got back to the Wick, I wanted to go straight to bed. To my surprise I found my new neighbours watching the telly in my room. I think they must have concluded that I was a one-off visitor and having left no belongings had just scampered. They were over-apologetic and shamefaced. It took me some time to reassure them that I wasn't put out although I wanted to sleep. I found myself overdoing the smiles and showing admiration of the four little ones none of whom spoke any English and then there was Ishmael, a lovely looking wide-eyed teenage boy if ever there was one. I decided not to do the obvious white man thing and ask, as if interested, where they came from, were they refugees or asylum seekers etc. Instead I asked if Ishmael if he was hungry. He immediately put the palms of his hands up and furiously shaking his head from side to side, managed to say no, no, no. It was handy that he didn't want my hospitality as I brought some takeaway Chinese, with some spare ribs and other bits of pork and prawns mixed in. Along with the wine I don't think they would have been able to enjoy any of it. I didn't ask but I assumed they were Muslims and by their colour, from North Africa. Anyway they were settled in to a Simpsons DVD and I gestured that they should watch it through. Meanwhile I got on with setting up my new laptop, lusting after my dinner. It is ironic isn't it, I had decided not to pretend interest in their story, so to make things relaxed I end up suppressing my hunger in order not to offend. Ishmael watched every move I made with the new computer. I could see the longing in his eyes to touch and as soon as I got it up and running I let him hold it. I thought he would never let it go, when his mother came into the room, her head covered, and she didn't look me in the eyes, acted as if I didn't exist. She summoned them and they all obediently left the room. Ishmael parted with such an engaging smile as he gently handed back my machine as if it was a holy relic. Once they had gone I gobbled down my food drank the wine and fell asleep watching Newsnight.

Day Three

It was raining cats and dogs when I eventually woke. For the first time I used the kitchen. It was scrupulously clean. All the pots and pans and cutlery were in place. I had to make my coffee in a saucepan. And although I had the feeling that I was being watched, whenever I turned to look there was no sign of anyone except the last time I heard the family's door fasten. It became a challenge. I set myself the task to be eventually invited into their small room. I went to an Islamic-looking shop nearby and resolved that as soon as the rain stopped to go and buy some Arabic-looking products and leave them around, hoping I could feign culinary incompetence and get my co-habitees to cook and thereby get closer if for no other reason than mutual convenience and perhaps a journalistic angle. They were as quiet as mice. I felt like their jailer. I tried to resolve the situation by moving the telly into the kitchen and putting on a Simpsons tape as loud as possible. Knocking on their door I closed mine tight; it worked. The mother's voice got louder and sounded a bit cross, in the end she gave in and they were soon chirping away in the kitchen. When the rain stopped I knocked on the door and the mother came to the door and I uttered my pre-planned words, 'Could Ishmael accompany me to the shops and help me carry some heavy shopping?'

This was a rather comical experience as I mimed the sentence and as I went along she agreed immediately with a knowing smile. I assume she understood every word yet she ordered Ishmael in their language to accompany me. Once outside Ishmael became introspective, even a bit frightened, he glanced here and there as if he was being observed. After a while he adopted a proper manner, you know, like when you are out with your uncle or auntie on a trip to London. I hoped he would relax and make the whole thing easier for me. Eventually we came across a Halal grocers and I set about filling my trolley, while Ishmael hovered by the door. As you know I have a tendency to show off and I bought rather a lot of stuff. Those shops can be expensive, the large can of cooking oil was over twelve quid and the bits and pieces and some meat found me spending over fifty pounds. And this is the strange thing, after struggling to get if all back to the flat and with me indicating that it was for everyone to share, you know, my generous contribution seemed to go down like a lead balloon. I bet most of the stuff is still there today. The kids wouldn't even take the sweets. Only Ishmael signalled thanks and that was rather like a prisoner breaking rank and chumming up to the jailers whilst trying not to be noticed by the other inmates.

My plan now was to assume my identity as a journalist, knock on every door in the building stating that I was researching the local feelings of those who live in the proximity of the upcoming Olympic site and their opinion of the effect on Hackney Wick of the actual Olympic event. Eventually, with some legitimacy I would knock on the Flee Man's door. Clever, eh? Well, I thought so at the time. I knocked on three ground floor doors before I got my first bite. A tall, thin, shaven-headed 'Peter, Peter Mann' from somewhere in Eastern Europe, an extended nose and a furtive manner invited me in without hesitation. He was the most contrary person I've met for a long time. I wouldn't bother telling you about him if I hadn't been alarmed that he might well be a serious sex offender and Jennifer, if you got time, you could, should have him checked out. I'm not trying to load you up with things to do, but what with the little children upstairs, you know! I first asked this Mr Mann, 'With the Olympic site being so close I've heard it suggested that some of the locals feel that they haven't had a choice in the matter.' A fact I had read some time ago in the Guardian. 'I...I thought I would call round to ask your opinion.' I think he suspected I was an official of some sort who had been sent round to check him out. He invited me in to his musty abode as a formality. I followed in to a dark front room where I guess the curtains are never drawn. He was watching a sex video of an Arabian woman being shagged by two huge - beyond natural-sized - cocks, the poor thing was pretending that she was enjoying it; I could sense that my host certainly was. He indicated for me to sit down and join him in his ogle. Out of politeness I pretended to be interested for a while and then tried to steer him onto the issue. As if bowing to the demands of petty officialdom he switched off the tape; before its climax. (If there was ever to be one.)

He basically said he didn't give a fuck about the Olympics and that it wasn't his country and as long as he was left alone the rest of the world could do whatever it wanted to do. He had seen it all coming from where he came from (I never found out exactly where). All human beings want is somewhere to sleep and someone to screw and what was wrong with this country was that we let the immigrants, Jews and blacks run everything.

I noticed some pictures of very young girls, of all colours, stuck on the walls; when he saw me looking at them, he clenched his right fist and put his left hand on his right arm muscle and grotesquely simulated sex - or rape, more like. He grinned at me as if I naturally shared his cock-thrusting fantasy. He had one of those smiles which confirms that nobody in their right mind would want to have voluntary sex with him. As I wasn't getting anywhere fast I asked him if he knew the guy in number eleven. That stopped him in his tracks. 'That black nigger bastard, years ago he pulled a knife on me when I told him not to park outside my window; playing music in his car so loud that my fucking windows shook. That's what's wrong with this country, fucking pimps. I heard the same row again the other morning. He must be back.' 'OK,' I said and left. I just worry that he's there and what he might be tempted to do. At least I had found out that the Flee Man was now likely to be in. Oh and I casually asked on leaving did he know the Smiths. He said within a heartbeat, that he was Badger's favourite 'specialist mechanic'. I didn't ask him then what that meant but I found out later. I had feared that he had a large cock and used it on who knows what for the Smiths' sexual thirsts. It turns out that 'Peter Man' (get it?), which was his adopted name, is an old-style criminal name for a safe-cracker. The telly was on in the kitchen when I got back, just buzzing away, the other guests hadn't changed the programme. It felt a bit spooky, I went over to their firmly shut door and put my ear to it. I couldn't hear anything. I was feeling some sort of nagging responsibility for what yesterday hadn't been a problem. After all I couldn't say that it was none of my business; and now somehow it was. It just worried me that Mr Sex Mann was downstairs and the sweet little innocent North Africans were like a temptation to him and they're so vulnerable. I had moved the telly back into my room and I typed for a bit, before entering a deep sleep for half the night and then a dream-driven, furtive blanket-wrestling, light sleep for the rest. I woke in a cold sweat and found that I had completely forgotten the subject of my nightmare; but was shaking with fear nevertheless.

Anyway, there is a point to what I'm telling you. Whatever the outcome, I feel that somebody/ you should know the nature of this - for the want of a better word - 'set'. A cozy arrangement that lives and breathes in the twilight world of Hackney Wick, a Badgers' set no less. The next evening I got myself invited to a 'do'.

Day Four

I discovered that all the occupants in this block had in some way or another links to the Smiths. A four-storeyed council build which the institutionalized criminals now own lock, stock and barrel. Apparently bought with help from the Public Purse and nowadays stuffed with their grace and favour retinue. Some artistic types met me again, as I returned with more shopping, they cornered me, before I could get my rehearsed patter out; flouncing up on me they chimed together, 'We have heard that you are a journalist covering what we think about the Olympics, you can ask all the questions you want to at the annual Party tonight as everybody in the block would be there.' News gets out fast.

I got there before everybody else, bad habit. The hosts are both full-time artists. Rose paints and draws in what you might describe as the modern conventional manner and Terry

Fanshaw-Smith is a distant relative of the main man. This born-again hippy has gained some sort of recognition for using as his subject matter plastic street barriers, you know the ones that you see all over London; usually in the very hole they are supposed to be protecting the public from falling into. Apparently he films them in situ. I put on my sincere face and went on about the bluer ones mean something quite different from the red and orange ones and should be considered as quite symbolically something else. He took me seriously. I bet he wants to do the Turner Prize thing. I didn't say anything but I think they've moved on from the sort of thing he does. He said he liked being interviewed. What I did say to him was, 'I've been told that a dangerous man lived in the flats,' and, 'Do you know the Flee Man personally? I believe he lives upstairs.' He shrugged nonchalantly, and waved his hands in front of him, as if to say, 'So what?' By that time we had been joined by Czech and Slo, two charming gay men who, unsurprisingly, hail from the Czech and Slovak Republics. Conveniently from a border town where they had set up a printing press and art gallery, would you believe, with the Smith Charities Foundation money. I can just imagine it has a double purpose. 'He lived upstairs before he went to prison and his room has been left undisturbed all this time. Which I think is a sign of trust. Don't you?' So boasted Czech, who followed on with a storyteller's flourish and getting into the subject, added, with a exciting sense of intrigue, 'It wasn't until two days ago that I heard him turn up again in the middle of the night in a wonderfully loud car, bashing out throbbing sounds from yesteryear. He went straight upstairs and I heard him lock his door.' Slo changed their mood, he put me wise with, 'Are you aware that the Flee Man was a convicted murderer as well as a police informant, who had originally entered the country on an illegal passport and had been used by his police handlers to infiltrate a so-called gang of Yardies and their phantom crack and cocaine empire?' and 'Do you know it's a well recorded fact that after the long years of Police activity that the prolonged investigation turned out, the so called Yardie threat was a fiction.' It went off like a gossip competition. It was told to me as if it all had often been spoken out aloud before. Czech took up the baton. 'Or was it?' I saw him throw a meaningful stare in his partner's direction. 'The Flee Man is credited for having sorted them out. There was some doubt about who was on whose side.' It came out later that a number of the Jamaican gangsters had been run by the Immigration officers and their friends at the Home Office. I pretended to lose interest and jokingly asked them. 'How many has he killed so far and was he likely to come to the party?' The last bit made every body laugh.

This is why I am relating this to you, Jennifer, as accurately as possible. Rose said in a concerned and formal way, from the kitchen in a loud and clear voice so that there can be no mistake, that she disapproved. 'He is said to have killed three women in Kingston and, while he has been here, another two. And before all of you think that that is enough, he is also said to have pushed a young boy off a roof top of one of the local tower blocks. All of this while he was being run by the Drug Squad! Now that somehow he is out again I suppose that he will kill more women. I would have thought that they would have deported him. I can't imagine that that they have further use him,' she fumed.

I didn't say it but if he was until recently in prison he couldn't have killed Auntie Yvonne. Unless they had let him out to do it, it's certainly confusing. She went on, 'I haven't seen him yet and I hope I don't. I thought something odd was up the other night when I distinctly heard a gunshot.'

Again, I didn't say anything. But I was finding it very easy to get answers to easy questions although they didn't add up. As the event wore on it became clear that Wayne and Winston had made a film there some months earlier. I suppose my interviewees were relaxed and thinking, again that their off the cuff opinions, being freely expressed were sanctioned by the Chief Beast. Otherwise, I wouldn't have been there, been allowed in. Yet I must say I was surprised by their collective frankness.

Perhaps they were practising coming clean at some official investigation. On the other hand, I feel they felt immune, safe and protected and they liked to celebrate their notoriety.

I met 'Old Frank' whose decades-old relationship with some Rastafarians provided him with a living selling proper sun-blessed Ganga. In an Ancient Mariner grip he told how he and others in the past had systematically looted the Hackney Town Hall of its treasures that had lain in a bomb shelter in the adjacent car park. What made if so funny to him was that nobody to this day has said a thing about the theft as the staff had turned over so often they were unaware that there was anything missing let alone that its treasures have been 'lifted'. It proved something to him. I think he wouldn't have liked at least to have been challenged. Everyone seems to hate the local Council as hopeless time fillers. He sells his weed in one of the ground floor flats, it's said that he has local police clients. The quality is that good, as is his reputation for giving the precise weight; they have made him into a local institution. There was a bubbly girl who worked full time for the Smith charities and said precisely her scope was from Aardvarks to Zen, all under the blessing of St Anthony the Great. 'Why him?'I politely inquired.' Because that is what Mr Smith requires. He has an interest in St Anthony who lived in a cave in the early days of the Church.' she moved away. Another said he was an electronic engineer and could tell me if I had the time how never to pay a power bill as long as I live. Two demure and very fancyable black girls, I found out later were high quality whores, busily chopped up the coke. There was even a couple who worked in the dole office. I imagine they sorted everyone out with their dole and housing benefit. Oh and a trio of Lady Boys who proudly declared as if adding value to their desirability 'we're all illegal entrants' (geddit?). I got close to Rose and asked how it was that Ishmael and his family were living in the block. She said that the Smiths have a certain relationship with a local mosque and from time to time helped out. Just before the music was turned up so loud that conversation became impossible I met the other side of the Smiths largesse. A huge skinhead type approached me declaring that he was the London convenor of the Celtic Soldiers of Christianity and that I should keep everything that I had learnt to myself or I would be talking directly to my own bollocks. 'Just a friendly warning and no harm intended, mind.'

I left as the whole room jumped up and joined in the Madness 'Our House' turned up full volume. It was their ritual moment. I went downstairs and found Ishmael sleeping on the floor by my bed and the telly on full blast. I didn't disturb him but lay down on my mattress and tried to fit in to my mind what I had learnt. Eventually I got up again and jotted down the notes you have, I hope, just read. Tomorrow I am resolved to attempt to interview the Flee Man. If it's any consolation apparently he only murders women. I feel ashamed that I have just written that down. If it's true that he is still in the hands of Home Office or Immigration officers and now they have let him out again I can only assume that he is being monitored.

Somehow - is it for a dare? - I've got to ask him what he knows about the mysterious death of Auntie Yvonne. Quite honestly I am shitting myself in anticipation. I plan to wait to see him arrive or leave and approach him on the stairs. If I don't catch him during the day I will knock on his door later in the evening. As I was earlier typing I have been joined by Ishmael who sits patiently by my side. In the middle of the night I woke with an erection and noticed that Ishmael beside me also had one. We were both surprised and I think we both blushed. Fortunately he left the room.

Day Five

The next day I managed to persuade Ishmael's mum to cook us lunch, he stayed in his room and the little children ran around with squeals of happiness and I kept my wary eye out for the Flee Man. At last I was invited into their tiny council flat room. It wasn't a shock that they had so few possessions but what did disturb me was how tidy it was. Considering that there were two little boys and two little girls, Ishmael and his mum they had worked out how to survive in such a confined place. Ishmael took the role as the man and welcomed me and indicated we should all sit cross legged and eat, other than that there was no formality. As we sat there I heard some very loud bass thumping car music and noise on the communal stairs. I told myself it was time to ascend the stairs and meet the man. A half an hour later I left my new friends, after much excruciating difficulty I managed to give them £100 of your cash. I know you would have done the same. I knocked on my quarry's door a number of times before eventually a voice called out wanting to know who it was. I told my name and that I was journalist and that I had come to interview on a matter of mutual interest. Several locks were undone and heavy bolts dragged across the top and bottom of door before it swung open. No one in sight I stepped gingerly in and was instantly grabbed in a headlock from behind and then pushed into the middle of the room and onto a bed. Although the room was dark I could make out the personalities of, yes, Tom, Dick and Harry or as they're properly known Detectives Onobolu. Mendes and Flanagan.'What the fuck you doing here?' the short African grabbed me by my throat. 'You're interfering with police business and I have a good mind to lock you up.' I managed to gasp, 'You're up to your neck in criminal business and I can prove it.' He released me helped me sit up. The tall one even straightened my jacket.

'Go on then, tell us what you know, or what you think you know.' They sat themselves around me on the bed, adopted phoney interested faces. The assault had left me panting, although out of breath I pointed out at a rapid speed that they were in league with Badger Smith and his family, supplied drugs to the Royal Family as well as having drugged me that they were, de facto, here in the home of a well known murderer. I speculated that they knew exactly who killed Auntie Yvonne. That they were interfering and perverting the course of justice, were acting in their own interests. I concluded by accusing them of being rogue cops.

My diatribe didn't impress them. The obviously intelligent one, Dick, explained in a mock childlike manner, slapping my face in a gentle fashion, and asked, 'Have you considered that we have been authorized in our pursuit of various villains?', and added that I was sticking my nose in much further then my face will allow. I had provided them with quite a predicament. One, what were they going to do with me now? Two, how far could I be trusted, three, should they report me?'

Sitting in the middle of them on the bed, quite an acrimonious row broke out between the three of them. I could see that my fate lay within their often hostile argument. When you read this you might well have clues to my eventual outcome. I shall stick to the names we have given them - or as I believe Patricia described them. Harry was the shortest South African looking one; Mendes I believe his surname is. 'Bet he would like to beat the fucking living daylights out of me and that nothing good could come of letting me carry on with my bullshit.' He went on with quite a racist rant, comparing me with the duplicitous, white, motherfucking men the world over, as well as being a middle-class cunt etc, etc. I'm not sure who he thought was worse. If I get found at the bottom of the river it might well be Harry who put me there. Tom, I think Flanagan, very tall and with a faint Caribbean twang mixed with an East London background, had a different perspective. He said that I should be handed over as quickly as possible to 'The Man' - I presume that meant his/their controller. He reasoned that I was too well connected to be dumped or locked up on minor offences, which wouldn't stick anyway. He thought that once I had got my big mouth started it would create difficulties for them.

'Even though Patricia and Dave were a departmental joke they were officially linked to the case or cases that they were involved in.' He concluded by saying that they were in enough trouble anyway and having got this far, didn't want to blow it all on a wanker like me. He threw his hands up in a gesture of frustration.

Dick, Onobolu then, the thinker. He too included me in his summing up of the situation. He said that I must have a 'purpose', as it was his working philosophy to use whatever card is dealt to him. He insisted that they should not react in the dumb way that the other two seemed to be suggesting. The fact was they were stuck with me and it should be taken into consideration.'That I had made myself known to the others in the house.'

At first he thought I could be used as some sort of 'patsy'. He went into a long silence as he thought it out, paced the room holding his hand out as if waiting for inspiration. Every now and again Harry would jab me with a karate move; at one time Tom had to restrain him. My mind filled with dread. 'Patsy?' Whatever would that mean? I saw myself left in this darkened room to be discovered by a convicted murderer who on his return would, to say the least, be put out to find me there. Dick looked at me directly again. This time I could tell he knew the answer. 'You have got to be of some fucking use!' I was also formulating some sort of answer. I didn't get a chance to say: perhaps, I could act as look out or just quit the scene. 'I would swear on whatever bible that they choose, to quit and they would never hear or see me again.'

Quite honestly, darling sister, by that time I had quite literally had it and was ready to chuck in my quest. Dick said, 'We would be wise to call the Smiths and say that we have with us here, this dude. Someone at the party last night will have already let them know. He had no doubt that I had shot my mouth off about being a journalist. I've heard that already from three different sources.' He went outside for a while. We could hear him talking on his mobile. As soon as he left the room the three of us went silent, although not letting on to each other, all strained to listen to Dick's call. I got the feeling he was describing me and I distinctly heard the word journalist. He came back in, seized centre focus and, in a take it or leave it manner, laid out the options. He said he had talked to both the Badger and his press officer. They were interested in my Olympics questions and were prepared to meet me in the late morning on the following day. The three of them would take me to his 'compound' in Potters Bar. He confirmed he had told them I was a journalist staying in one of his flats. He had not linked me to my other connections. 'So my options are to meet the man himself or fuck off for good. And never be seen or heard of again.' The other two weren't sure about letting me do this. Dick's the boss and wins the day. 'They would call for me the following morning and if I was there; so be it etc.' They quite clearly expected that I wouldn't make the roll call. It was agreed, I left them in silence and went back to my room.

I'm finished writing up my description of my goings on so far. All of a sudden I am having an amazing exquisite mental dilemma. Should I just opt out, I think no one would mind a teeny bit, or should I carry on with this hopeless façade? Let's face it this Auntie Yvonne Caribbean lady wouldn't have given me the time of day. I seriously doubt that I could have ever moved in her circles. A fish out of water would be too generous a description of little old me, eh? Yet my fate, my cross roads, my only claim to living outside the box, impressing you as well, hopefully, is finding out about her, of whom I know so little, and why she's now dead. I am working on this hypothesis. Some years ago according to various websites the Police with the help of some journalists set up the now infamous Yardies crack cocaine myth. Eventually it all came out in the wash. It turned out a lot of taxpayers' money had been spent on a phoney set up and the State had to reluctantly put its hand up too setting up illegally imported Jamaican hard men, many of whom were psychotic killers. The scheme was to lure out the locals and nail them. The Flee Man was probably a double agent who embarrassed the authorities by murdering women as a sideline, while being an illegal immigrant managed and sanctioned by the Home Office. My question is why and who would want Auntie Yvonne out of the way? The answer must surely be that she knew too much.

It could well be that the Flee Man has either been released or transferred to a soft option prison, prior that is to deportation and, true to his name, has done a bunk. On the other hand it is said he had been sent to Jamaica where he murdered Auntie Yvonne. Yet he could even now be back in operation working hard for some one. So it could well be true that he killed her at the request of whoever and one day when his use is up will on re-capture be sent back to Spanish Town Jail as a certified madman. The one thing that sticks out a mile is that there are numerous hands being played by interested parties.

Badger Smith has stuck his snout in since the beginning and from what I have learnt could have anything illegally done whenever he wants it done. Obviously there is a cover up going on. My hunch is that Tom, Dick and Harry are the Smiths' syndicate's local police where they walk a tightrope on either side of the law. If Patricia hadn't inadvertently triggered interest in the poor lady's funeral it would have all passed by and we wouldn't be asking the question. I believe that our sudden interest has disturbed the camouflage and there is rustling in the undergrowth. What is about to be revealed, whatever it is, will not be popular and there will be many who would wish it would all go away.

Since I got in Ishmael has kept a sort of shadowy presence in the room. I could see that he could see I was troubled, contemplative, you know! He sat out of sight as I ate some food that his mother must have prepared, he is still here. Well, darling sister I can and can't imagine what you will make of this tract. As your irritating half-brother over the years I have witnessed much of your life and to tell the truth and conscious that it's a cliché to say, I have lived in your shadow too. You and your mum and two dads. We all know that my dad was a write-off as an intellect, preferring mushroom farming and old cars. But your old man actually inspired you to try out things. He tried too hard, that's why your mum dumped him. So as you picked up his baton we all held our breath. In the middle of all that European philosophy you stunned us all then by marrying David. A man who the word plod was invented for, anal retentive mind, an organic 'square' just not 'YOU,' Sorry...I have tried recently with the help of Father Ignatius to become friendly with him. As the years rolled by we entered this weird dance, miles and miles of spoken words whirl by, all about very little. We hide our purgatorial unhappiness in the façade of interest in the arts. Showing off how current we are, about what's after all, is sanctioned by the Sunday Times. We are in danger of becoming acutely boring. You so wittily paraphrase Google and say, 'Cyber-space's availability heralds the end of mystery'. Does that let you off the hook? I beg to differ for I'm now not in a safe world. It's all becoming a mystery. I have tried to give you an unbiased insight into the different worlds I have entered. I have been truthful about the image I project to those whose world I have entered. Most of them I find are initially rude towards me. I am seen by them as middle class and somehow deficient – and even open to derogatory swear words. Yet as I learn to hold my ground I think I slowly gain respect.

I learnt a trick when I was sent to a state school on my 14th birthday. You let someone call you a cunt and you eventually look back at them and inquire what exactly their status is. As they usually don't want to answer, you've opened up the prospect that they might be a cunt as well. I know you object to the use of the word but it's not meant in the context that you put it in. People keep calling me it and I'm not a woman and they don't seem to be saying that I am. Nothing is what one supposes it to be and if you turn it upside down it makes just as much sense. I have those in my new reality at a disadvantage, for they assume that they know me and I let them. What is getting me out, away from my, 'go along with it all' past, is that I now challenge all assumptions. I am doing what you would really like to be doing - delving into the unknown... so there!

x Toby

Day Six

In a Stanislavsky type of method acting, I woke up and began taking on the persona of a journalist. I needed to feel the part. I went to the corner shop and bought a note book and some bacon and eggs, which on cooking must have been a culinary shock to my Islamic co-habitees, who I have never seen again. Tom knocked on my door and told me with an almost friendly chuckle that my carriage was awaiting. I took all my belongings and closed the door to that steaming, breathing and frightening house. My companions were on their best behaviour. Dick/Nigel quickly put me at ease. 'I won the bet that you would make it.'

Harry turned up the radio so loud and from then on I couldn't hear what was being said. Dick drove and Harry sat in the front; rather than conversation they would shout at each other and then follow up with loud sustained laughter. It was a bit disconcerting as I wanted to feel comfortable with my new character: Toby the Journalist. We whizzed through the electronic gate at the front of the Smiths' HQ, there we were in the beast's lair. It felt a bit like being in a foreign country. Like the Vatican City in the middle of Rome, different rules and regulations apply here. You don't have to be told you just assume it. We sat for half an hour in a conservatory type reception area resplendent with rare ferns and palms, a beautiful oriental receptionist and a whole range of up to date periodicals and a beautiful illustrated tome on St Anthony the Great in a glass case. The three cops sat away from me bent over in conversation. After some time a smart young Asian man led us over to the house, up and along corridors. I lost my sense direction and eventually we arrived at the back of a house and went into a barn extension. We were ushered in and straight into Badger John Smith himself. He beckoned us to all sit down and guided me to a single upright chair close to his desk. I could sense the three servile policemen sat on a settee behind me. I placed my lap top on my lap and opened my new note book on it, with pen poised. Badger looks both distinguished and aged well, manicured to the state of almost camp. He had wavy grey hair, trimmed beard, expensive glasses and I believe a hidden hearing aid. You immediately get the impression that he demands respect or else. Well into his seventies he is very present, alert and gives off an air of interest in what's going on. The room was decorated in a tastefully medieval style. Expensive and genuine-looking early Christian icons of bearded saints looked on. A strong mature London voice evolved through years of experience asked, 'Where did you spring from?'

Dick answered that I interviewed the tenants in the Hackney Wick house about the Olympics. That was enough, I was believed. Mr. Smith went on one, as they say. I took notes as fast as I could. Here was I hoping after a bit of banter on the 2012 Olympics to get quickly around to asking him what his considered opinion on the Auntie Yvonne question was. Instead I was hearing full blast about the bastards who are up to their elbows in it.

Basically, he went along with it in the beginning, the Olympic planning, helping councils' compulsory purchase of buildings etc. Legally cleaning them out of dubious tenants that couldn't stand up to the court costs. Or didn't fancy facing up to his 'always legitimate, mind' bailiffs. He was all for co-operation with various regeneration schemes, which he labouriously listed. He preferred that type of joint investment as it was efficient and didn't need all that dependence on elected members to sanction every detail.

This method of doing business had been encouraged by Governments and up to the economic crisis 2008 and 2009 he felt he had been shown the green 'Go' light. He clearly felt he had now been gazumped. He felt he held the dice and as a player expected to win sites and hotels on this local monopoly board. In a roundabout way he found out there was a totally different game being played. He was still very cross. The side of his neck turned a scarlet hue as he described how he had financed a local boxing club. They promised that the locals would get involved. 'Who's more local than me?' He boomed. 'It's a fix, an establishment fix like that fucking Dome business.' He pointed his fingers at me as if to inform me of a heinous crime.

'They use every fucker's money and then go

broke and bail it out and then hand it over to their mates. And we all sit there and buy it! Oh, changed its name then to O-fucking-2? Oh, it must be alright now then! £98 million later; is that all? Okay then... And now the Olympics is a three-card trick played by the State on us all. Now you see it now you don't. We put our money on the card and hey ho they own the developed site when it's all over. And the punter is expected to grin and bear it.' I managed to squeeze in, 'Won't we all enjoy the spectacle?' He looked at me with sympathy.

'Yes of course there will be excitement and the public will no doubt get turned on by the events. Let's hope we win lots of medals.' He seemed irritated with me that I hadn't taken on his point that he had been pushed out of the Establishment's inner circle, which was gobbling up the financial feast without him. Had I realized in the recent economic crisis, 'That through various streams of liquid funds he has at his finger tips, helped save the fucking country?' So obliged was the Bank of England that they had sent envoys to consult with him in the middle of the last financial crisis. He ended this bit of his discourse with the promise that if I wanted he would supply me with the details of the double dealing of the Olympic mafia. He would have various documents sent on to me. Imagine all that illegal cash rolling around in the Smiths' orbit and him wanting to invest in a public spectacle and Caesar won't let him. I thought I could get him on the subject of criminality by asking, 'Why keep your cash liquid?'

He said that he didn't know what I knew about his business and as far as he was concerned it wasn't the point of the interview. He then went on to describe the stock exchange and its brokers as the real criminals in society. He embraced globalization and had investments around the planet.' But these thieving bastards put nothing back. I run charities alongside my enterprises. Those buggers wouldn't give you the drippings off their nose.'

He was proud that he was above politics and relished the fact that all the parties from time to time seek out his opinion. At that he indicated that the interview had run its natural course. Pretending to look at his watch he said he had given us a half an hour.

'So I must thank you lads for bringing this fine upstanding journalist to meet me.' At that we all stood up and as he went to shake my hand I slipped in, 'Do you think that the Police had used the Flee Man to execute the local lady known as Auntie Yvonne?'

At first he didn't seem to hear me and was patting me on the back with one hand and shaking hands with Dick with the other. We were all walking away from him towards the door held open by his man. 'What the fuck did you say?' he roared.

I was about to repeat my question when he got hold of me and propelled me onto the settee. He squared up to the shuffling cops. 'What are you fuckers playing at? Where did you get this toe rag from?'

Dick mumbled a bit, then went on to say that he had been trying to tell him exactly that. There were a lot of questions being asked about this murder. And that I turned up at the house asking about the Olympics and Auntie Yvonne so they had brought me here so that he could hear for himself. 'What? What?? What??? What the fuck have the Olympics and that old coppers' nark Yvonne got to do with each other?' He was now in the middle of the room addressing the gods in bewilderment. 'You knew her then?' I chanced. 'Every fucker knew her and she knew something about everybody. I don't know or care who killed her. You are an insolent little fucker and I've a good mind to introduce you to some Kiwi friends of mine to teach you some manners.' He suddenly changed tack and adopted a more executive pose, 'Perhaps while you are here you could tell me what else you know about my association with the deceased?' The cops stood by the door holding their hands in front of them and held their breaths. I could see and feel their discomfort. I wondered if this is what Nigel Onobolu had wanted to happen. Like a schoolboy witnessing the headmaster catching red handed someone he had set up, he nervously laughed.

'I know that you kidnapped the wrong woman and that your purpose probably was to cover up some of your well known and recorded nefarious activities. If as you say you had nothing to do with Auntie Yvonne's death then you've got to admit that your involvement needs explanation. Doesn't it? With a reputation such as yours you can't be surprised that there is interest... Can you?' I had stunned him and you could see his mind working. I thought I had calculated it right. I could hear my heart beating like a bass drum. I felt sure he couldn't assault me in front of three police witnesses however compliant they might be towards his wishes.

My plan was that once he knew that I was aware of his twilight world he would become more at ease and be prepared to discuss the matter. Even he was going to cover up his involvement. I wanted to ask in his opinion: did she know too much and was her murder linked to the phoney Yardie debacle? Then it all went pear shaped. 'Where did you say you found this cunt?' he demanded of Dick. 'He turned up in the flat that your charity runs for the Mosque.' 'Don't tell me that they let him in. Who let him in?' 'Winston and Wayne I suppose. They met him outside your Port Royal Club after they had met up with the Kiwi Twins... I think they had a room there.' That was it: the Badger went into an incandescent rage.

'No wonder that little cocksucker feels so full

of himself. He has been listening to those two wankers. I hoped I taught them a lesson and by now gone back to their neck of the woods and joined the church. I bet you think you know a lot about our business. Well, let me put you straight sonny boy. That what you might think you know is not worth shit. You are playing with words in a big man's world where actions speak louder, much fucking louder. Do you get my meaning? Do you?' He shouted directly into my face and I found myself nodding in humble agreement. 'Who put you up to this, that's what I want to know. I hope it wasn't you lot. I know in the end I can't count on your loyalty, but this isn't it, is it?'

Tom, Dick and Harry were dumb struck. Hear no evil, see no evil and certainly speak no evil. 'Well, what are we going to do with this cunt? Chop him up? Chuck him in the canal? Like they used to do in the good old days?' It felt like a mock threat. Dick told him that I was relative of David who was Patricia's police partner and that they had been justified in bringing me along because I was poking around and that they had believed at first that I was working on behalf of someone else. He needed to witness himself that I existed, but now he realized, I was a joke. Yet I should be seen as a warning, that there was interest in the Flee Man and Auntie Yvonne. He then turned to me and said that I had been disrespectful to Mr Smith and that I should apologize and indicated with his eyes that I was getting off lightly. It was an amazing feeling to be threatened and yet knowing that I was going to walk out unharmed. Without Badger's okay, we bundle out of the room. As we left the Asian bodyguard pushed up against me and Tom pulled me though. They set a fast pace anxious it seemed to leave the compound before all hell broke loose. We left by a different route and entered a big room, and there, would you believe, sat Maggie, Patricia's sister. 'What's happening?' asked Nigel. 'I'm here for a job interview,' she coyly replied. I think those two have something going on. He forced the pace of our exit. We got in the car and as the gates opened and as we sped along the road back to town they started laughing and slapping each other's hands.

'Was I your patsy?' I asked. 'You could say that,' said Tom. He pulled over into a layby switched off the engine and turned to me and told me in all seriousness that I should quit while I was still alive. Nigel added, 'It had been useful for them to present me to the Badger and in a way I had been their patsy as they need a working relationship with him because he was a major player and that one day it was their ambition to nail him; but not yet.' He said he knew I would put my foot in it but in the way of things I had played a role and that I should go away for a bit and leave it to the professionals. Particularly if I didn't want to meet the Kiwi twins who will without a doubt be looking for me.

I got out of the car, having learnt a lot; I came home and fortunately you weren't in and I could type up my notes. I'm not sure if we will unravel the Auntie Yvonne mystery. I certainly won't as I will be in Australia or somewhere. I fear that the Badgers' friends would seek me out and teach me some of their manners if I was to stay. Maybe I will write a book about it all. I feel that my intense experience in the last six days have changed my attitude to the world around us. It hasn't hurt me to ask questions and I know that when you read this you will be envious that I have at least had walked on the wild side ….for a bit

Love

Toby xxx

Recording Transcript 12

"Hi feeling any better?"

"Sort of."

"One would hope that a week off would be just that."

"How about you?"

"Terrible."

"Do you want to tell me?"

"I've been storing it up."

"Go on then…. you first."

"Jennifer's brother Toby has done her head in."

"He looked all right that time I met him. He seemed interested in my problem. I felt flattered. Quite a nice chap, you may say. Talked in a proper manner."

"Well, he has taken her money. Gone to Australia after spending a drug crazy week in one of Badger Smith's Hackney Wick houses. He left a detailed journal. If you can be bothered to read it, he comes across like Norman Wisdom, putting his foot in everywhere he went, every move he made. Worst of all being used by your Tom, Dick, and Harry mates, as bait to the Badger Smith."

"Who is Norman Wisdom again?"

"A lovable clown who failed to make me laugh."

"So Jennifer must be freaking out."

"And some. What's got into him I don't know, silly fucker. Thought he could blend in and find out clues to what happened to your Auntie Yvonne. Claiming he was a journalist he must have stuck out like a pork sausage in a mosque.....and what's worse, she blames it all on me and you."

"I didn't ask him. I didn't ask any of you. I've got my own problems...Look there he is ... Mr Crow going into his nest...Nice suit...anyway I'm at a loss with my sister. She has left our flat...Maggie's gone."

"Toby in his notes says he saw her at the Smiths HQ looking for a job."

"Isn't that just too terrible. She actually told me that they had rung her. What's got into her? Her parting words were that I stifled her, just like our dad had and she hardly knew Auntie Yvonne, thought my interest in the case was morbid. On top of that I was a copper and in her world everyone hated the racist pigs. Finally she said I was regarded locally as Auntie Tom."

"She has never taken her half brother properly. He did though, he walked in her shadow. I got fed up with him. I've tried recently along with the Priest get on with him. I don't mind telling you I'm glad he's gone. She has gone off her rocker."

"I've had to put the kids upstairs with Mrs. Constantine and that's going to cost real money."

"The Priest has got involved. Toby copied his notes to Father Xavier, who's recently taken it on himself to get involved. He's gone to Hackney Wick to look at the house that Toby stayed in. He was stern with her freaking out distraught sister act. He told her she should be pleased that her baby brother had intervened for the common good and that it was a positive move. He seemed inspired himself. My quip that it at least got Toby out of the house wasn't received well."

"The last thing we did as a family was to go to a reception in Wins Snooker Hall in Chatsworth Rd. It was full of community types who we have known for years. The talk was of who was or wasn't owning up to cutting back their lifestyles because of the recession. You could tell everybody feared for their jobs, you could feel it in the air but they weren't letting on. We're all having a good time despite it all was the common message. Maggie sat apart all night long. I asked did people mind that I was a cop? They all took the piss of course. I could now tell the truth, you know? From knowing them all so long, while they will open up and concede it's a novel twist for a black woman to be a cop, it still came home to me that they don't like thinking of me as a policewoman. Hey ho…Ok I am listening. The wife's flipped, the Priest rejoined the world and the Boy Wonder has left it."

"Our days are numbered."

"Did he learn anything helpful?"

"Well, the Hackney Wick house is full of criminals of one sort or another and illegal immigrants. Oh and Leroy Stuart the one and only Flee Man has got the penthouse, which Toby doesn't seemed to have met despite trying. Two boys he met outside the Port Royal,

Wayne and Winston, were the ones who molested Maggie, introduced him to the place in fact."

"What do you mean, we've had it? Our days are numbered?"

"Jennifer is rarely wrong."

"I need the overtime."

"I need to get out of the house."

"If we have got nothing to lose why don't we go and look at the Wick crime scene?"

"If for no other reason than to stake out a real crime scene, I agree."

****

"I'll pull over here. We can look up the street from here. I think it is the block in the middle, by the street light."

"This is a bit of a walk on the wild side for me...doing a bunk. I don't fancy we should stay here too long."

"You won't have to...There's your three coppers rushing into the building, a bit fast."

"Just look at them go."

"All of a sudden they're here and inside. Something's up."

"Is this your Priest coming up the road, talking on his mobile phone? It is him, isn't it?"

"Oh shit. What's he up to… straight into the house... Look!"

"And now the tall cop has come down the stairs on his phone. I can hear sirens coming."

'Yes, and here we are, sitting in the middle. It's obviously a big deal. Is it too late for us to move?"

"Are we stuck here? I think we are. All we can do is sit it out."

"They are putting out crime scene tape at each end of the road."

"Two ambulances."

"Here come the other tenants out to take a look."

"Inspectors and Suits and a couple of plods taking command of the front door."

"Crime Photographer and two in whites."

"Occupants ushered into the street. It's a big one."

"That looks like a Big Chiefs' conference being held on the path...look over there some Somali looking family melting in to the night, up they go to the end of road. Under the tape they go."

"They've got through…They won't let the tenants back in for a while…Toby claimed the whole building is chock-a-block full of quality grade Charlie."

"Here we are sticking out like a sore thumb, there look, here comes a plod checking car numbers."

"What will we say?"

"That we saw a man who looked like Bob Crow go inside...let me think."

"Don't take too long. Look at that Inspector indicating to the others that he will walk up here."

"Wind down your window first, so that he has lean in over you and me."

"Why?"

"If he is uncomfortable he won't stay too long."

"Let's hope so."

"Do it now, signal him, that's it......Good evening."

"Inspector Durant, Hackney's Finest here. For what do we owe your august presence? Special detail, down this way? Is there something we should know? How long have you been here?"

"We're waiting for my lodger. The Catholic Priest who I believe is inside now helping with the investigation. We saw him go in just as we arrived."

"Does your Command know you're here?"

"They will. ... mind your head."

"Stay here won't you?"

"He didn't seem too put out. Will we be in trouble?"

"I will get Jennifer thinking about it. Anyway, so what? I know it in my bones that we are on the way out."

"Well, this ain't going to help."

"There go your men."

"Tom, Dick and Harry, no less."

"Friends of the Royals, friends of the criminals, friends of Maggie's, oh yes, who else I wonder are your friends friendly with…?"

"Okay… Here comes your man again, I will do my window this time. Keeps things flexible."

"I'm afraid I will have to make a full report. There seems to be other links concerning you both that will need checking out. There is no reason to detain you any further and I suggest you piss off back to where you belong."

"The Priest?"

"Oh, he said that he wasn't expecting you. So I suggest that you…"

"Can we know what's up?"

"Two young black males brutally murdered. Please don't talk to anyone. I will know if you do."

"Thanks, goodnight."

"I was going to say that I live local… sharp you were. I wonder who the dead men could be?"

"I think I can guess."

The Priest's Letter

My Dearest Jennifer,

You say that you have lost your faith in me. What does that mean? I have told you I have no faith. Like many others I now trust in 'reason' which as any fool can see doesn't always explain itself easily. I now spend my life, often in the dark, working out reasons for why things happen. You called and charged that I had betrayed you yet you don't say how. I'm not sure what makes up your faith. Is it another ambiguous English word that you use for effect? There are two murdered young men Wayne and Winston and our beloved Toby has fled, quite literally the scene of the crime. What are the reasons? You ask am I still your friend? I am and will always act with your interest in mind. Please be reassured. When Toby first entered the Hackney Wick apartments he sent me texts, which included Wayne's mobile number. Shortly after Toby went incommunicado, concerned I called the number several times. Eventually Wayne answered with a text. I had explained that I was Priest, a friend of Toby and asked did they want to talk. It worked and we agreed to meet in the

Rose Garden in Regent's Park. They didn't turn up, or they watched me from a distance. It is convenient to be still dressed as a Roman Catholic Priest and strangely I find it open doors. After a few days I received a text from them giving me an address in the Mozart Estate off the Harrow Road where Wayne and Winston had much to tell me. They were extremely fearful. Now they're both dead. I was listening to your message as I arrived at the house in question. I had been called by Police Detective Onobolu who had found my mobile number from both of their cell phones listed as PRIEST and would I join him in a very important police investigation. Apparently the last text sent was for me, giving me their new address. Which turned out to be their last. The door to the top left hand flat had been kicked in and there were a number of bullet holes. I would say that a small machine gun had sprayed the door and there were bullet holes in the hallway wall behind me as I entered the flat. Both of the men had bullet wounds on their bodies and I imagine after a fierce gun fight they had been executed. Onobolu asked me to confirm that I knew the deceased and sadly looking at the shocked and distorted bodies, I could. They wanted to know why I had been talking to Wayne and Winston. What had we talked about and what had they told me?

'It was between the deceased and myself.' I said. A Detective Mendes sneered, 'I expect you have been hearing their confessions.' This was useful because I could now look each of them in the eye in turn and say, 'What is told to me is only between myself and themselves.' Conveniently, one of them added, 'And God's'.

I changed the subject indicating confidentiality and I wouldn't budge. Instead I told them my link had been Toby. Quite surprisingly they all groaned. I explained how I met them, how Wayne and Winston seemed to be in fear of certain people, that they both had 'in good faith' named them to me. It struck me as odd that at the time these investigative police detectives, didn't ask who exactly those were. I decided to be careful with these unusual policemen, as they had also been mentioned as dangerous enemies by the deceased boys.

Instead, I asked, 'Do they have an idea who would have killed them? They used one of those British sayings that test us foreigners. "That would be telling wouldn't it?"

Which means more than no but means not necessarily a full yes. Onobolu took me aside and told me in confidence that he was concerned that I was linked to other people who he said were sticking their nose in.

As we talked a dozen or so crime investigators filled the room. Still dressed as a Priest I was shown respect. A high ranking Inspector asked had I experienced anything like this before. I told him that I was from Rwanda and that I was on leave from active duties. He became very understanding towards me and said he was sorry. Sorry to me, about the young dead in front of us. I felt like saying it's really nothing to me other than the worthless horror of it all. I had liked the young men and they were educated to some sort of a standard. Sorry is an over-used word in this country. 'Yes, I'm sorry too.'

You're right when you tell me it's not like where I come from. The tribal conditions in which thousands are slaughtered are not transferable to a society divided by extreme wealth as this is. As you have often said,

'Everyone in this setup knows where they fit in the pecking order or they're too stupid if they don't.'

There are those in my homeland too who have accumulated too much wealth; here it is stratified, endemic, institutional and rock hard. Yet you call yourselves free. Your Government feel free to bomb other countries and you can't stop them. Mothers mourn their dead soldier sons and the city morgues are full of dead unemployed youths. Everywhere criminals live like fleas on the society and its difficult to feel sorrow when they are crushed. Two more is a statistic, sad but true.

In my previous experience some around me called those they shared their homeland with 'cockroaches'. Motivated by pernicious indoctrination and the narrow economics of tribal power they debased themselves and mercilessly massacred their neighbours. I went beyond sorrow. If there was any belief left in me, it vanished then. I wonder if I ever told you I was already in doubt about my faith, years before the disaster. I could then see we had no plans for a post-imperialist Africa other than to prostitute ourselves to the selfish and greedy West. I belonged to a church that couldn't intervene for the general good. It was as ever on both sides but mostly on its own. What could we say to our devoted brethren other than to say, have faith?

For a long while I tried to be anonymous. It now seems that my entry into your society is helped by looking like a Priest. It seems to open doors in a way that other immigrants couldn't find as easy. I wonder if I am a coward and hide behind a mask. I won't lie about belief or giving false blessings but yes I let the clerical appearance work for me. This contradiction is after all who I am. I don't know who else to be.

I know it's such a short while from when I was suicidal. I feel I have travelled a hundred years since then. I will always carry the cancer of my past with me, there is no escape. Now after nearly two decades of depression I feel compelled to move on. With you as a confident I feel free to communicate again.

Jennifer, I have taken your advice to heart. You counselled that I should reach out and so I have. I will investigate this uneven society and find out it raison d'être if that is at all possible. So then, Toby wrote to us that he had discovered that the psychotic murderer Leroy Stuart lived in the top floor apartment, where the murdered young men were eventually slain. Was this man involved in their deaths? From what I learn about him it seems likely he played a key part. I reiterate the Police didn't mention him which made me all the more suspicious. What were their reasons?

Toby was attempting to find out who killed David's police partner Patricia's Auntie Yvonne. He was also concerned that the three policemen of whom I recently met were involved in a suspicious way with a criminal businessman, a Mr John Smith. These policemen seem to be licensed to roam East London at will. They deal in drugs as we have heard. They have 'popped up' I think that is the right expression, in every aspect of the story so far.

It was unknown to me at that time and I imagine you also, that David and Patricia were, in police parlance 'staking out the place' in Hackney Wick. Imagine my surprise when an Inspector told me that they, David and Patricia, were waiting for me in the street. They are, you say, in jeopardy.

I imagine they will be even more so now as they were obviously working on their own initiative.

I didn't encourage Toby it was the other way round. He was, in his own words, stifled and decided to do something about it. I am sure he will be back one day full of more interesting observations. Meanwhile I will stay away from you until you find yourself able to talk to me. You accused me of just running off and jumping in at the deep end. In other words, leaving you alone, to use a British expression, you should grow up.

Jennifer's reply

Grow up! Grow up? What kind of advice is that?

What is happening? I have only myself to ask. The three men who were living here have buggered off and left me. Like the classic cliché I am becoming the fretful little woman left at home while the menfolk do what they have to do. Toby has, after years of being an irritating appendage, lifted the garbage lid of society and is surprised at what he saw there and has now fled, taking my money with him; to who knows where. My so-called husband, who having spent most of his life being duplicitous for a living, now threatens our security by going off the tracks or is over the other side of the track sticking his nose into East End gang killings all because his so called partner wants to find who killed her auntie - not related, mind you - one Auntie Yvonne.

What does David think he is going to do? Infiltrate the gangsters too? Don't make me laugh, If only I could laugh at it all. He rarely comes home. He'd rather stay in Police barracks than in his own home. I expect, any day from now, to hear he's moved in with that suitably dull woman Patricia Murray.

The children change their mobile phones and don't tell me their new numbers. On top of these you have had a sudden change of heart parading yourself as a active Priest while helping the Police with their inquiries. After years of hiding in darkened rooms frightened by your own shadows, you have joined my other so-called house mates and have become sleuths, dabbling in the murky and dangerous criminal underworld.

Well, you shining knights in armour don't expect to find me waiting for you when you return home with your tails between your legs – that is, if they haven't been cut off. Grow up, you say? It's you three who should, I think, grow up. While you and Toby aren't under orders, David is. Already I've taken 'off the record' phone calls from friendly superiors. Just wait till the unfriendly ones go after them both. As for you out there in the London jungle, I wish I could pray for you. But I don't have faith either. I can only hope that you remain cautious. If I don't see you ever again, good luck.

Recording transcript 13

"Good morning."

"Hi."

"How's tricks? Anything new happening in your life?"

"New! I wouldn't say that another row with Maggie was new."

"So she is back then?"

"Back with a vengeance. The Smiths kicked her out and she is blaming us. They said they didn't like us snooping around. Badger's son gave her another £500. Made her sign a receipt and then cancelled a flat they were going to move her into. She blames it all on me. It's like talking to a kid. I pointed out that it was them who kidnapped her and messed about with her after all. She screamed at me that it had been me they wanted to talk to in the first place. I can't win. She claimed that the murder of Wayne and Winston was also my fault because your brother in law Toby had hung out with them and asked too many questions. She was told that they had been killed by the Flee Man. All this wouldn't have happened if her sister wasn't a fat black policewoman who blabbed her business to your family who've nothing better to do with their lives than go poke around in others lives. Et cetera, et cetera."

"What a fucking mess."

"I'm still no wiser about who killed Auntie Yvonne or

why. As for Maggie, I get the feeling that for all her anti-police mouth she is sweet on one of those Tom, Dick and Harry characters. I think it's the smart one Dick. I said she could move back in if she gets a job, she slammed her bedroom door and didn't come out, I could hear her playing on her Nintendo all night. I've just about had it with her."

"Jennifer has gone mad, threatened to burn the house down last night when I passed by. She fears for Toby. She even has a theory that Toby might not have left and has been killed by who knows who. The Priest has left his luggage there but has been gone for days. She says he is roaming around Hackney in his Priest gear investigating who killed Wayne and Winston and chumming up to the top brass. She thinks he could be the next victim. I had to promise that I would stay there every night. If I did she wouldn't burn the house down. I hate to see her so distressed."

"Do you still have any love for her?"

"That's a very difficult question... I sometimes wonder if I ever did love her. I'm an appendage. I bring my share of the money home. Marriage or at least mine is like walking with a permanent stone in your shoe, one that you have got to get used to. Live with come what may. Now that the kids have gone... you know. Anyway, I promised to be good boy and go home."

"Isn't that something you trained to do?"

"What?"

"Well, you're good at pretending, you know, you're used

to living a lie. I mean when you were spying on people. Letting all of them think one thing about you, while all the time you aren't what you seem. Isn't that it?"

"Doesn't everybody do that to some extent? Sometimes I'm sincere. I prefer to be, if it's at all possible."

"Well, what do you think I should do about my sister?"

"Well, what do you think I should do about Jennifer, the Priest and Toby?"

"I don't know."

"Well, I don't know either."

"I haven't got a clue."

"We're both clueless…great detectives aren't we?"

"Maybe we should ask Bob Crow."

"Yes that's an idea. I've seen him on telly a lot recently. He always seems to know what he's talking about."

"You sleep first and I'll sleep second… okay?"

"If you insist."

****

"Jennifer rang while you were kipping. She wants us to join her this evening at McGinty's Goat, a restaurant off the Kilburn High Road. I have been there before. Great big portions of Irish stew, steak, lamb chops, that sort of thing and wooden cubicles. We can hold a private conversation in one of them. She has some important news and she means it. Apparently there's a VIP who it's essential for us to meet tonight. It's kind of official police business and she wouldn't say any more than that."

"OK ...I suppose. How come they call her?"

"All will be revealed. Knowing her I am sure of that."

"At such short notice it better had. I will need to get Maggie to babysit. I might even have to pay her. It better be worth it."

"I have a feeling it will. Actually when I think about it I can read between the lines and guess who the very important person will be. You're right, why would the department ring her? It will be her friend Malcolm Sutherland MP, the Tory member of the cross-party Home Office Police Committee I bet you. I think we are in trouble and he will tell us why. I've been feeling it my bones for some time."

"Do you get on with him?"

"No, not at all."

"Do you think it has to do with us being outside the Hackney Wick crime scene the other night?"

"Maybe, I've got a nasty feeling, had it in my bones for days. He has never come out in the open before. We are about to learn our fate."

5. Transcript of recordings made at McGinty's Goat Restaurant

"Here we are…. If we sit opposite each other up the end against the wall, they will have to talk at us as one. Don't stand up to greet them when they come but invite them to squeeze in and join us."

"You've been here before?"

"Not that often…I know the pitfalls of two conversations going on at the same time. You don't all get to hear the same thing at the same time, and find out later there's two agendas, or one was told this and the other that and then the other finds out later on and its to late to compare notes. You know?"

"Yes. I live and learn from you. How was Maggie?"

"We're all right now, we made it up. I expect she been adding up the numbers, weighing up the pros and cons. She's a smart girl, or to put it another way she's smart enough to know that I would throw her out of my house if she didn't start to give back something in return. There's got to be give and take in a relationship if it is going work. Talking of which I just saw a reflection of your missus. in the reception mirror over there, wearing her orange coat, let me stretch a bit so I can see… Yes it's her. She's standing in the front bit. She must be waiting for someone. Quickly tell me about this MP again."

"He is in with the Home Office, specialising in the Metropolitan Police, a member of a standing cross-party committee for a long time. New Labour, Liberal Democrats and Tories, they're all in it. It's a watch committee monitoring the Police. Probably giving them political advice and feedback. You can imagine they have some say in things... Here they are..."

Come in and join us Patricia, you've met Jennifer and this is Malcolm..."

MS = Malcolm Sutherland MP
JT = Jennifer Thwaite
DT = David Thwaite
PM = Patricia Murray.

MS: You must be Patricia, how do you do? Oh this is a squeeze to get into.

JT: You should eat less Mr. Sutherland, hello again Patricia.

PM: That goes for me too.

JT: And me, we've probably come to the wrong place then.

MS: Come off it Jenny you're as thin as a rake, isn't she David?

PM: Known each other a long time?

DT: They do, they go way, way back. We all do.

MS: I'll tell the waiter to hold on for a bit. I'll say we are waiting for extra guests and to come back later. I've taken the liberty I hope you don't mind, of bringing this recording machine. As, for one, I would like to be able to establish that we have nothing to hide and I imagine you all do too. I hope you will not be too restrained by its presence. This is an unusual gathering, albeit off the record. It could be open to some misinterpretation and speculation. Who knows? And none of us will want that will we? No, I will turn it on at a mutually agreed time and let it run. Its only use is that we have an indisputable unedited record of our conversation. I will of course provide each party with a copy on request. (To waiter) Give us ten minutes old chap we're waiting for some others.

JT: Is all this necessary? Why don't you get to what you want to say and say it?

MS: Well then, where to start? Let me cut to the quick. You two seem lately to have wandered out of your area of duty. Jennifer has been informed, and other sources also report, that you have been spotted outside an East End crime scene. One that has nothing to do with you, other than, I understand, Patricia here, has a murdered, shall we say, a non-relative, relative. One Auntie Yvonne I believe her name to be, or at least how she is referred to. Yes? Good. It also seems that this link came about though the misinterpretation of DC Murray's – Patricia, that is - interest in the said non-relative's funeral. Let me at this point put on record that I know both DS Thwaite, David that is, and Jennifer Thwaite, who have been married to each other for some time. And let it be noted that I also know Toby Rudge, Jennifer's younger half brother who has, I am informed, also attempted to unearth the killer or killers of PC Murray's non-relative...

DT: Auntie Yvonne.

MS: This lad has, according to his sister, unearthed certain matters of interest. His disturbing report, although unsolicited, came into my hands; thanks Jennifer. And I can assure you that appropriate parts have been sent to the relevant departments and I expect to receive a response in due course. Now let me emphasize this, I have been advised from on top, so to speak, that your intrusions quite frankly haven't been welcome and indeed could well have jeopardized ongoing investigations. Now why I think that this meeting is necessary is because there is this other matter that I will need to explain my involvement in. I will explain the crossovers as this meeting proceeds.

PM: Am I not permitted to look for the killer, or killers, of my Auntie Yvonne, the 'non-relative' you have just now referred too?

DT: Cut to the chase Malcolm!

MS: Cut?...OK.....Your Department is about to be cut and you have four weeks left that is if you're not immediately suspended. There, now I've said it. It wasn't as hard as I thought it was going to be. The reason why I am telling you all this is precisely because we all need to show that there is nothing up our sleeves, so to speak. The fact I am a friend of the family and a member of the Cross-Party Home Office Standing Met Police Committee has some bearing as it is at the request of the

Committee that the surveillance programme, of which you two are a part of, exists.

JT: Ceased to exist.

DT: So he told you first?

JT: Why shouldn't I know, it's my life as well?

DT: I knew it in my bones anyway. It's never made sense. You would have to be born yesterday not to have realized that Bob Crow was already a target for political surveillance from numerous agencies and that having a car in plain view, permanently parked outside the RMT union HQ and even more so his home was a complete waste of taxpayers' money; to put it in context.

MS: Please don't raise your voice. We don't want everybody in the restaurant listening in. Well, I agree that some of what you assert might be true. However others have argued that visual presence is of mutual interest almost as a diplomatic courtesy that the Met should have an ongoing relationship with the RMT Union albeit at mutual arm's length has value. They officially know that we are watching them and they can't be surprised if and when this comes into the open. Whilst the contradiction in all this is that the stake-out crews as in your case weren't properly equipped and were basically token. I can't help thinking that we, you, have had a good run.

PM: What kind of run have you had?

DT: He's been shagging my wife while I'm sitting in the car with you watching somebody they don't like.

PM: What? …When? …Was that the motive all along? I thought you said it was about politics.

DT: It is, as well. After all, the establishment still fears organized labour or in this case re-organized labour. So the excuse is to warn them that they are being watched by having us watch them in the open. The joke being we were ill-equipped, I mean unequipped to do anything anyway but be a pawn in the age old game.

PM: What are you actually saying? So he could sleep with your wife?

JT: You're so crude David, always have been …Patricia it's rubbish…"

DT: And you have always been up to something.

MS: Can we please lower our voices? Let's remain good humoured, if for no other reason than those who might be listening hear that that we held, are holding rather, a comprehensive and thorough discussion in which all interests are declared. David, joking apart, I can assure you that my friendship with your wife has always been on both a professional and a personal capacity. It would be quite wrong of you to assert that this relationship was in anyway other than proper. So let's move on to other matters.

PM: What the hell is going on between you all?

MS: I reject any notion that anything untoward has happened between us in this or elsewhere. I'm beginning to sound silly now. It's time to switch this thing off….

JT: Wait a moment. What about the Priest? Isn't he to be recorded as well? He is due to be present soon. I expect him here shortly.

MS: Too late, I've switched the bloody thing off.

JT: Malcolm! Please put the tape machine back on.

MS: If you insist... as long as David doesn't make unhelpful jibes

DT: Even if they're true.

PM: So we're just pawns.

MS: Yes - well, no. I'm not sure how aware you are of the ins and outs of the political world.

JT: Don't be too condescending Malcolm.

MS: Okay, yes, in a way, we're all pawns.

DT: Some more than others.

PM: Why don't you start at the beginning?

JT: Please be brief; Malcolm has a tendency to elaborate.

MS: Through all the years of this blighted New Labour Government, it has been a sensitive issue that far from being partners, the Blair and Brown Government distrust each other intensely. In fact any Government lives in fear of strikes and whatnot. New Labour is no exception. While on the one hand it can be argued that in recent years the unions have been contained, laws on balloting, picketing, secondary actions and so on, as much as we all wish it, they haven't gone away. Take the Olympic Park development for instance. Wildcat strike action there now for instance could put the boot on the other foot. Encourage sympathetic militancy, and so on. On the other hand certain elements of the Labour Party now wish to pose as pro-union. By having a, yes, token, visual surveillance, the Met could claim to being doing its duty and placate any awkward questions by avoiding the accusation that its other methods might be, let's say, improper even illegal. This low-cost policy was considered to be of interest in keeping the media at bay. While it can be said nowadays it only seems to be interested in celebrities and terror suspects, if they had a hint that we were vulnerable they would cook up a storm. To put it frankly we don't want to be exposed as negligent by the Daily Mail whose readers think that Bob Crow is the Devil incarnate.

DT: And who are fascinated by misbehaving MPs.

MS: It's all over now and can be hung out to dry, as outmoded so to speak. What with a new Government about to be elected, Patricia, the problem was that year after year the budgets have been clipped. What with the advent of terrorism 9/11 and 7/7 and so on, skilled officers were given new priorities etc. I'm sure you understand. I will declare that I recommended David for these reduced surveillance activities as I knew he wasn't usefully engaged at that time but had a surveillance background. There is nothing improper in that.

PM: And what about me? Where do I fit in?

MS: From Parking wasn't it?

DT: I've known it all along.

PM: You could have told me.

DT: I met you at least.

PM: Yes that's true.

JT: I thought as much. Let's order.

Arrival of Father Ignatius Xavier = IX

JT: We all know Father Ignatius Xavier don't we? As you see Father we are all eating very nice steaks. Shall we order for you? Meanwhile why don't you bring us up to date on your investigations? Malcolm is making a recording of the meeting so be careful what you say, do you mind? As you were mentioned earlier in our conversation our mindful MP wishes to keep the record straight. An English analogy meaning above board or nothing to hide.

IX: 'Whatever', as your young ones say.

JT: Well done!

MS: Oh…. Okay then, why not? Please be brief.

IX: I have been following the theory that Leroy Stuart is the killer of Yvonne, whose second name I have yet to learn…

PM: Lawless, Yvonne Lawless, Auntie Yvonne… Lawless.

IX: Thank you. It is said that Leroy Stuart has since killed two young men Wayne and Winston. It has also been pointed out by the Police that he might be wounded as well and gone into hiding. I checked Homerton Hospital and am working my way through to other local A&Es. I let the Hospital authorities think that I've been summoned by a wounded man, although I don't know who it actually is. I then ask does anyone fit that description. I feel sure they would have told me. I don't believe he has been at the hospitals at all. After all Leroy Stuart is known as the Flee Man for a very good reason. The opposite positions are: (A) That it wasn't this main suspect Stuart who was shot back at through the flats door; or (B) whoever it was who fired at the lads, was not hit. If, whoever the perpetrator was, fired first having persuaded the victims to stand by the door and could have known their visitor or visitors and were put off guard. Quite probably they were completely surprised by the attack. Although they were hit they could have returned fire; yet the assailant or assailants could have ducked away before kicking down the door and then executing both the wounded men. I returned the next day, the day after, you two, had been outside the victim's apartment some hours after the killing. I decided not to take the Police warning. They told me not to involve myself. Following Toby's description of the inmates in the Hackney Wick property, owned by the known criminal John Smith also known as the Badger...

MS: Just to interrupt - I feel I must ask does his fascinating spade work involve me in any way? If not, I could switch off the tape recorder.

IX: Only that I gave your name as a reference to the Police when they asked me to confirm my identity.

MS: Oh really! Okay? You better tell all…

.IX: Leroy Stuart is what one might call a quadruple agent. He has worked for the British Home Office and Immigration authorities. The Badger Smiths. The mysterious Yardie gang that seemed to have more double agents than bona fide members. Including of course whoever it was who sanctioned him in Jamaica. I think, as you say, he has been playing both sides at once or, as you might say, many sides at once. The question must be put, is he still active and if so who is he in touch with, working for, or is he embarked on a lone vendetta? Will there be other victims? It seems you all understand that three people can be labelled in a manner if they have something in common. As it is, with the three policemen, who you all call, Tom, Dick and Harry; a derogatory joke I think. Well, these three detectives, Onobolu, Mendes and Flanagan should be taken very seriously as they are as you say, 'Up to their necks in it.' Toby records that he was with them in the crime scene apartment some days earlier. Prior to that they had placed him in Wayne and Winston's care, after they had drugged him. They claim that they are pursuing the Flee Man Stuart and were waiting for him in his home. Do they know who the killer or killers were? How involved are they? We know that they have a close relationship with this Badger Smith man and his crime syndicate. We must ask; did they kill the two? Thinking perhaps they were dealing with the main suspect, after all we must ask what were Wayne and Winston doing in the main fugitives' flat?

MS: You know I do think it's time for me to go. I'll just stretch over and switch off the machine. And squeeze out. There we go and let me put this £50 note into the pot and say goodnight....Goodnight very interesting but must get back to the House.

JT: Are they sitting this late?

MS: Oh no.....I sort of have a meeting. I will be in touch.

IX: Good night to you, Shall I continue?

PM: Yes. For me, yes.

DT: It's good to see you with your teeth into something.

JT: Oh yes. I think you must.

IX: Well, it's about time I reveal to you that I am collaborating with Al O'Connor as well.

JT: What? ...Al who? ....Oh no, that waste of space. No I don't believe it. I just don't believe you would both use me.

IX: It's only fair David that she knows. I think we have recorded what you needed. You've got what you want.

JT: What! Who? What? Did you say? Al O'Connor? Why?

IX: He told me how well you know him.

JT: Good bye then I am out of here now... you bastards ... I am sorry Patricia... I guess you're not one of them, you twisting bastards. You pathetic sods.

PM: I'm going too.

6. The Truth is out and about: Letter from Aloysius O'Connor

Detective Onobolu,

You wanted it in writing. Here it is.....I come clean. Here then is an account of my last few days in England in the new General Election month of May 2010.

It's me. I did it. I organized the bugging of David and Patricia Murray's surveillance car and I also put Jennifer's brother up to his snooping activities. Well, what I actually did, was to strongly hint to him that it's about time he did something imaginative if he wanted to affect his moribund situation. I suggested I would monitor his report and that it would help me as well. He seemed to want to get involved; jumped at it. Lift the lid. I was surprised he went as far as he did. Some of what Toby found out gave me a new insight into the interconnecting world of London crime, adding a whole new dimension to my scheme. Okay, financially I motivated the Priest, which again wasn't as hard as one would have thought, taking all into consideration. The big one is that you forced me to own up to is, I confess that I planned with David Thwaite to create, manufacture a scandal using a tiny recording device. A bugged trap for my quarry to fall into, a scandal that I want relentlessly exposed in the media as soon as you agree.

At first I fancied a banner headline,

Tory MP bugger bugged

or, if not 'bugger', then,

Tory spook spooked

or,

Top Tory MP used privileged Home Office Committee post to cuckold police spook

Malcolm Sutherland, the senior Conservative MP, has been caught with his pants down. A hugely embarrassing sting operation has revealed that the Surrey Central MP used his influence to keep an expensive stake-out car outside the RMT Union leader Bob Crow's London HQ, while he dated/chased a hard-working detective's wife.

That was my first draft. Next I fancied something like,

Cross-Party Home Office Police Committee Tory has been exposed as middleman in crime syndicate investigation.

MP Malcolm Sutherland tipped to hold a Cabinet Post in a future Conservative Government has been accused of using his influence to halt ongoing Metropolitan Police investigations. The MP has become involved in a covert operation concerning the gangland slaying of two young East End criminals. It has been claimed that Sutherland has conducted off the record meetings in a Kilburn Café where he met surveillance officers concerned in the case. It has been alleged that he informed the said officers that they were to be dropped by the Met crime team and

were not to involve themselves in the ongoing murder case despite their breakthrough investigations.

Responding to the breaking news Scotland Yard today confirmed that any unofficial contact between serving officers and Home Office police Committee Members concerning any ongoing investigation would be considered a breach of procedure and could under no circumstances be sanctioned. They would launch an immediate investigation. Tape recordings of this and other related matters have been widely circulated to the media.

Or,

Further revelations link sacked officer's wife with the disgraced Malcolm Sutherland MP. It is claimed that he influenced the deployment of a surveillance Category Five 'stake-out' vehicle to spy on a Union Leader. It was officially sanctioned by him and self-interested orders were put into operation at his request. It is claimed that he was behind the unnecessary activities so that he could liaise with the wife of one of the undercover officers. He is on tape agreeing that the surveillance car was token and was in place to placate media pressure.

This could go on to,

Sutherland's Committee-sanctioned spooks tailed Royalty to a late-night 'club'. It's also claimed that his Home Office committee had to be aware that the notorious underworld criminal Badger Smith and his family, owners of the shady late-night haunt the

Port Royal Club, were given police protection by a second closely linked Home Office investigation team. The sensational revelations bear the hallmark of police irregularity. Independent police monitors have suggested that these actions must have been sanctioned by the cross-party committee chaired by Malcolm Sutherland and if so are strictly against the rules.

We might even read,

Home Office stymied as killer kills again. Suspended Police officers linked to the mysterious murder in Jamaica of Londoner Yvonne Lawless whose investigation has been suddenly shelved. Double agent MP Sutherland was briefed on the links between the two teams and the murky East End drug world were frequent. How much did he know?

Nigel, this was the last one I wrote some days ago; I am waiting for the right moment to release the avalanche of information.

With Eton, Oxford, Guards and MI5 and MI6 contacts, Establishment, old school One Nation Tory, Malcolm Sutherland MP who has advised Conservative Party Leader David Cameron on future Government Policing Policies. Waiting in the wings for the widely anticipated incoming Conservative Government, the recently exposed Sutherland must now be agonizing about his uncertain inclusion in any future Cabinet. As an avalanche of hostile facts emerge claiming to reveal his double dealing the seriously challenged MP has yet to comment. Accusations of his improper

behaviour and self-interested activities have exposed the inner workings of the privileged Standing Home Office Police Committee which will now be clearly seen as not fit for purpose by the Government. The disgraced Sutherland resignation is expected soon.

Not soon enough for me, Aloysius O'Connor. Al to my friends, which these days are few. Don't worry, I don't count you as one.

Before I go out to meet the Priest, Father Ignatius, I will lay this one new fact on you. While it must be plain to you that I intend to bring Sutherland down by any scandalous means available, as you see, if I could somehow also blame him for Auntie Yvonne's murder, then I will. After all it was the Home Office that originally sanctioned the Flee Man and if my target can be tarred with that brush then I will stick it on him without hesitation.

The truth is that I doubt he is in fact screwing Jennifer. I believe, if he is sexual at all, he is gay. Which if he is, he had kept hidden. He certainly was when I first met him in Glasgow. Despite this fact it's been my intention to accuse him of arranging the stake-out duties so he could sleep with Dave's wife Jennifer. For me the truth is irrelevant. It's the sort of story the scandal rags will want to believe. The more evidence I make available and provide the better and if it snowballs into an avalanche then I will go home happy. Dave has always suspected that there was something motivating Sutherland to arrange the token 'stake-out duties'. It might even have been just a favour for Jennifer; whatever it is, it's deeply resented by her husband, who like me, wants to topple the man who has played an unwelcome role in a lot of his past life. We can prove it was all irregular and sex sells papers. I have been waiting for the moment to fire my shots. The laugh is that the stake out was cover against media exposure of inaction and now the boot is on the other foot and it will be seen as a waste of the taxpayers' money in these hard times. I bet you're wondering how many other cost cutting decisions taken by the Met are a joke. It's what happens in all large bureaucracies when they start saving expenditure.

A few days ago I had the most stimulating conversation with our Dear Father Ignatius at the Royal Institute of British Architects cafeteria in Great Portland Street. He is still a priest, it comes across as you talk to him. The only difference is he doesn't believe in God. One still finds oneself consulting him in a reverential manner, while he adopts a parochial pose and in return you find he is counselling you. On top of all that he wants payment. I have to constantly tell him my resources are limited.

I went in fast; asked why the fuck had he blown my name in McGinty's Goat. I pointed out that it wasn't in the plan to tell Jennifer at this time; particularly in that way. And as I was actually helping him out financially he should be loyal to me and the deal we made. He bounced back in a parable-delivering manner. Almost preaching, 'We can learn that when we upset the apple cart it is wise to save the horse.'

I pointed out it seemed to me that his primarymotive was indeed too keep in with Jennifer. I complained that I didn't like anyone selling me short. He shrugged it off and said that she would find out one way or another that I was back in the country, meeting up with her family, with a mission to bring down Sutherland. He thought it wise that he should be the one who told her, rather then the newspapers. We begged to differ and went on to talk about you, Detective Onobolu. I told him how we had met and the agreement we had reached.

The Priest for his part chose the unlikely rendezvous to meet, as he fears being pulled in by you lot. He is convinced that you believe he knows where Wayne and Winston's films and records are. He also feels that it's – for the want of another word – his "duty" to serve the dead boys' wishes and here the Priest bit comes in handy for him. He isn't open to challenge as he was now on his new chosen path.

I hired a car and with some difficulty found Hackney Wick. We drove past the Smiths' rented apartments. The Police have erected boarding around the outside and placed several large Met blue-coloured skips in the road. Piled high with rubble we could see and hear they were taking the place apart. Looking for Wayne and Winston's records; we both agreed. As we cruised along the A12 we saw various views of the Olympic sight I could imagine a thousand sharp deals had got it this far. We both gaped at the incongruity and juxtaposition of the new Olympic Land of OZ proportions set against the close by and co-existing run down jumble of warehouses and assorted dwellings that make up Hackney Wick. Situated just across the canal from each other, the billion-pound site ignoring the old Victorian warehouses made meaningful opinion near impossible.

Ignatius is in awe of the new East End 'jungle of architecture'. He warmed to his subject over an 'all-day breakfast' in a local greasy spoon: "It's a desperate ravaging profit-hungry capitalism unleashed on the once derelict east side of the Thames."

"The gigantic Canary Wharf is like a Norman fortress astride the river guarding the City of London from hostile competition. He fancied that the new razor-sharp glass buildings popping up here and there are postmodern settlements. Unlived in yet laying claim to the land at the expense of the deposed natives: "Windy corridors of powerful and prosperous non-residential ghosts." He claimed that the power that lights up the offices each and every night would suffice for the whole of Rwanda for a year. "Vengeance is mine, sayeth me," he eventually quipped. "I also sayeth me." "Ours, then," we both agreed. Let's get the bastards and shook hands. So now you know.

Up until then Ignatius had gone along with my plot without much query. It seemed that he had met Sutherland and hadn't liked his patronizing manner from the outset and had over time become sympatric towards David's plight. He saw how marginalized the man had become within his own family. Always a pawn in somebody else's game. For his part the Rwandan exile owes a debt to Jennifer yet feels she has manipulated the domestic scene to her own satisfaction at the cost of her family. Thankful that she befriended him, nevertheless the one-time Priest felt a bond with Toby, making it plain that he was seeing the lad's part in the unfolding story as a justifiable reason for his commitment. So here he was declaring he went along with my plan to sort out the 'links' we need to make; to do in the MP. I think quite frankly he has nothing better to do. He asked me, this late in the game. 'Why?' Exactly why was it so important to me? He took notes.

I told how I had been set up by Sutherland and Jennifer in the eighties. They had for their own interests set me a trap, landed me into the clutches of the Special Branch in Glasgow. I was tortured and beaten up – all in a day's work – by Special Branch policemen. Bags were put over my head and I was tied to a chair and pissed on. I finally was informed that I was being held under the PTA, the so-called Prevention of Terrorism Act. Sure I was sympathetic to the Republican cause and after Bobby Sands and the other Maze hunger strikers' deaths and the heartless Prime Minister Thatcher's disregard for their political rights I wanted to get involved. She consciously let them die in a hunger strike. When they were dead they then did deals. Anyone who had sympathy with the struggle in the North of Ireland felt incensed by the one-sided reports in the British media and the pig ignorance of your average Brit. 'They deserve each other,' was the ill-informed response of the public house sages 'If you ask me,' which they failed to notice nobody ever did, 'I'd drop a bomb on the bloody lot'.

Jennifer seemed sympathetic at first, even got out of me the little secrets that I knew. I told her things while we were having it off. I had a very close friend whose brother fired machine guns over the roof tops defending West Belfast. I boasted that his small active Republican cell had asked me to watch out for them in Scotland. In truth they had only hinted at it. For some reason I have never quite fathomed out why she told on me and in doing so somewhat embellished the tale of my exploits. Like many of the lads I was besotted by her. She was the best sex I have ever had. I don't know where she learnt if but she had a skill, she knew exactly what to do. Turn this way or that. Take your time. Hold on. How about doing it differently, how about doing this or that together? Do it again but this time try it with a bit more of self-confidence in your movements. She taught and I learned sheer sexual joy. I have never been able to pass on that satisfying exotic knowledge since, or experience anything else similar.

I told them everything I knew and more. I heard Malcolm Sutherland's distinct insincere laugh twice while I was incarcerated. I caught sight of him the day I was finally let go, bruised and beaten and abused. I always felt that they let me go as I had made up so much, it would cost too much for them to check it all out. Or that I had served a purpose as an example to the left straining on the leash during the Miners' Strike not to get ideas about armed struggle.

Jennifer eventually sent me a long letter saying how truly sorry she was and explained how she had also got into a lot of trouble. She didn't mention Sutherland. I rang David and we met in South Shields, he told me he had been a police plant in the Socialist Workers Party and that Jennifer blames herself for what happen to me. She had gone along with it all but realized too late she was being used. Used by Sutherland to get a foothold into the secret service. By setting me up he got a lifetime occupation. I bet that's how he got a seat in the House of Commons. She has been one way or another working with him ever since.

I think I can trust Ignatius. He has little respect for any powerful elite. He gives off a dignity which is combined with a searching intelligence and a fundamental honesty, besides he's got nothing to lose. He can never really belong in Britain. A free agent, a lost soul wandering through the land. The one thing he wanted to know was why I didn't want to bring down Jennifer as well. "All things considered," he queried, "By my account, she has played a major role in all the goings on. Shopping me to the secret service, manipulating David etc." I told him that David insisted that we leave her alone, for the sake of his kids. Anyway that was his condition when we met up and hatched our plot some months ago. Frankly though I could never see how she would be kept out of it once the shit hit the fan. And I don't see how he could have either.

You said that you wanted background, that you wanted to understand me. The more the better you said. What makes me tick. You told me what drives you. I hope it's true that we have common enemies. When you read this I expect I will have left the country. I'm writing this entry three days before the General Election on 6th May 2010. So here's my exclusive, for-your-eyes-only diary. It will be easy to do as I expect there will be a lot of hanging around as we count down to D Day.

As I say, I have told Ignatius of our unexpected meeting. I told him how you quizzed David after being informed by a furious Patricia about the bugging. How the spineless dolt shopped me. How you found me, how you pointed out to me through my locked hotel door that I had few options. That my game was up, or we could talk. How we eventually decided we were after the same thing and how feel you are being used to protect the Smiths. How Sutherland and his ilk provide the camouflage. Much of what I know and jot down you will have experienced from your side of the story.

And now what a story I now have to tell you about what happened since I wrote the above notes!

Ignatius is in custody. I have a bruised black eye and my hired car has been set on fire, I expect you know your erstwhile compatriots Detectives Mendes and Flanagan have declared war on us. They claimed that you instructed them to retrieve Wayne and Winston's records, films and tapes etc and if we didn't go along with them they would enforce seizure. Which I can tell you they did, well they think they did. Ignatius made the mistake of confirming that he knew where the murdered lads' recorded material was stored. We met your comrades at the Port Royal club at lunch time. It was the Priest's idea. He had called the first number he could find and got Flanagan. He presumed that you would be there as you all seem so inseparable. At first they were chummy and when I asked where you were, they both said that you were going to be late. I tested them saying I would prefer to wait for you. At that they got edgy, Mendes' attitude turned and he became the tough cop. As far as he was concerned I was in danger of wasting police time and could be arrested there and then if they saw fit. Suddenly Flanagan stood up and lent his face close into Ignatius' face. 'Have you got the fucking stuff with you? I told you to bring it with you. Is it in the car? Don't fuck with us!' He picked on the wrong bloke. Ignatius stood up and poked your man with his fingers and astonished us all. He addressed them both with a "now listen to me" authority. There is one tape I have seen where you are threatening Wayne and Winston with retribution if they don't hand over a film they made of you two actually delivering a consignment of packets to John Smith's house. It's quite clear on the sound track what you are all talking about. I believe that you didn't know that you were being videotaped by a concealed camera in their flat. It's all there. You cursed them, and told them that they should fear for their lives unless they handed over the Smith's film and tape records. Only when the boys threatened you with their guns did you leave. As I say 'it's all there'.

This was the bombshell.

'What do you want?' Flanagan asked us both in turn. 'Is it money? Are you trying to shake us down?' I was as surprised as they were. I hadn't been aware of any of this.

'Come on,' Ignatius grabbed me and we walked quickly out of the building and into the car park. With them hurriedly following on behind.

'Where the fuck do you think you two are going?' screamed a clearly frustrated Mendes. Flanagan grabbed me and Mendes tried to grip the Priest but he wasn't having any of this, he ran away. It was almost comical to watch as he dodged between cars. 'Come here you fucking cunt!' yelled the pursuing Mendes at the Priest. His yell was so loud that passers-by began to stop and wonder what was going on. It was as if they were playing tag. They both dashed around the Port Royal car park.

The agile Ignatius ran rings round his pursuer and around a big old Rolls-Royce saloon. Mendes was so frustrated he just couldn't lay his hands on the swift clergyman. One time Mendes jumped over the car bonnet and fell and landed on the gravel. A fascinated crowd of onlookers cheered, enjoying the free show without appreciating its desperate seriousness. For a moment, I thought Ignatius was sportingly going to help up the clearly frustrated foulmouthed swearing cop. He just stood there some feet away and teased him with a 'come and get me if you can' pose.

I saw my chance. I tried to break away from Flanagan's firm grip while he was distracted by the car park fun and games. He spun round and punched me in the eye. Well, I wasn't having that so I tried to head butt him and knee him in the balls. I missed both times. As luck would have it I managed to push him away, into an empty car parking attendant's kiosk where he lost his balance. The key was in the lock and I shut him in. I made it to my close-by car and drove at Mendes, who surprised by my speed darted around the other side of the Rolls. Ignatius seized the opportunity as I screeched to a halt and jumped into the passenger seat. As I accelerated away the furious Mendes threw off a large brick that bounced of the car roof. We zoomed past Flanagan's shaking shed, which now fell over. We laughed as it toppled over on to the door side making it even harder for him to get out.

'Why didn't you let me in on this?' I demanded of my exhausted panting friend. His answer was that he wasn't sure of you. He had long suspected the possibility that your companions were involved in the slaying of Winston and Wayne. Although I had previously had told him about our conversation, he said he had wanted to be sure that you weren't involved with the other two. I was visibly annoyed with him. I shouted at him that he had tempted fate and put us in danger. I said again 'That the least thing he could have done was to tell me what he was up to.' Not to leave me in the dark. In his superior way he actually uttered a dry laugh.

'This was the quickest way to confirm my suspicions of their involvement.'

'What if they had managed to detain us?'

'Then I would have done some sort of a deal with them. They are extremely anxious to get their hands on the incriminating material. Don't you think? We were in a public place. One where they are known, no way were they going to overplay their hands.'

'But they did.'

'Yes,' he did me the favour of conceding.

'I was surprised that they went as far as they did. They were pretty crude, weren't they?'

I had never seen him openly laugh before. He did again.

The fucker was enjoying himself. I had a black eye on the way and was now being pursued by two suspected murdering policemen. I couldn't for the life of me see the funny side. As we drove along Ignatius ruminated that Mendes and Flanagan were hoping to pin the murders on Flee Man Leroy Stuart and had quite probably killed Auntie Yvonne, who after all was a well known police informant and might have been aware of what these two had been up to. My concern was where we should go next and what to do.

'Where is Wayne and Winston's evidence?'

'I have no idea,' came the astonishing reply. 'I never knew.'

'Well, how did you know about the concealed camera and the armed stand-off?'

'The lads boasted to me about it. They were frightened though I could tell that.'

Driving along with the exhilarated Priest, a sudden feeling of foreboding overcame me. I seemed to be straying off course. Sure, bring down my lifelong enemy, implicate him in unlawful activities and destroy his grubby career while sticking my fingers up to the British Establishment. I now feared that my plan of stealth and sweet revenge was beginning to go off track. It's one thing to use the system's own methods of information gathering against them but quite another to have their goons pursuing me. So far I had built a case with plenty of stickable evidence. The new information has taken me further into Sutherland and his mate's twilight world. I can hint at leads, from the misuse of his privileged position and establish believable links with the underworld. Whatever its provability it's still strong enough shit to smear across the tabloid papers. But now? Now I'm reporting to you, a Met detective who I bet hasn't told my frantic pursuers that salient fact. For fuck's sake I'm being hunted by rogue policemen while in the company of an out and out chancer, whose search for the truth is, to say the least, provocative and unconventional.

I put it to the post-clerical sleuth, 'Couldn't it be, that it was the Flee Man who shot down Wayne and Winston at the behest of Badger Smith along with the murder of the phantom Auntie Yvonne, a police informant no less?'

'Quite possible, who knows at this moment?' he insisted.

'We are engaged with Flanagan and Mendes who I concede, might even be legitimate in their pursuit of the boys' records. It's entirely possible that they could be behaving in an aggressive manner because that's how they do it. Threatening violence seems to be a worldwide method of police interrogation and it always surprises me when the British are shocked that their own men do it.'

'Yes but I'm not.' I put it to him.

'If they are just doing their cop thing why don't we let them have the incriminating evidence and be done with it, a plague on both their houses? Or we could select the bits that reveal the Smiths' goings on and give them that and at the same time pass the stuff, that shows these two cops threatening the boys, onto my contact?'

Which, all said and done IS YOU, Nigel Onobolu!

The frustrating Father laughed his meaningless laugh again. 'I told you already I haven't got it.'

'Okay, but the rest of the stuff?'

'I haven't got that either.'

'Well, who has? Where is it?'

'I don't know,' I pointed out to him in no uncertain terms.'These guys are chasing us believing that we, you, have it and I don't think they are going to believe you, us, that is, that we haven't got it. Did the boys give you a clue?'

'All they said to me was that it was in the post.' 'What address did they have for you? Was it David's and Jennifer's?'

Believe you me I was getting frustrated.

'It may have been. The reason I am not clear is became I was moving about and was even thinking of staying in the Smiths' Hackney Wick apartment after Toby left. I didn't think at the time of my first contact with them that I would be getting mail from them. If it went to Hackney Wick the Police would have apprehended it by now.'

So you see at that point we didn't know where it was.

At one time during the above conversation I considered that Ignatius might have even been giving me the run around. He could have had several motives. He could have wanted to keep me out of it to protect me. He could have distrusted me because I am in contact with you. Or, he sees himself as a big player in his new found world of roaming detective. You know, Brother Cadfael meets Hercule Poirot.

We decided to visit David and Jennifer's house to check the post. I hid around the corner .while he went inside. He was gone a half an hour and when he eventually came back I asked what took him so long. He patiently informed me that Jennifer had a client and he had felt obliged to wait to speak to her; besides, he had to charge up his mobile phone. It turned out, while he was in there your erstwhile colleagues actually rang the house land line. Ignatius had answered it. As he was telling me this they drew up outside the house. Fortunately they didn't see us. We watched them get out of their car standing in the street looking over the garden fence. They stared though the windows for a long time, hoping I suppose to get a glimpse of us.

'If their inquires were legitimate wouldn't they knock on the door?' Ignatius wondered, and then without consultation, rang Flanagan's mobile and said that we would meet them outside the Smiths' compound. Immediately they jumped back into their car and sped by without noticing us so deep were they in conversation.

'A penny for their thoughts.'

'A penny for yours.' I was stunned. 'What the fuck are you up to?'

All he could say to my all too apparent anger was, 'We don't know the way to the Smiths so we had better follow them there.' Would you believe I obeyed him. 'What the hell are you up to?' I insisted. 'I am fast losing the plot and you are running away with your moves and dragging me – us – into more and more danger.'

It was difficult keeping up with the speeding detectives without them knowing that we were right behind them. A couple of times in the Holloway Road it was a miracle that they didn't look in their rear mirror and spot us. We both ducked down, at traffic lights, but they were so intent in their conversation they missed us. Ignatius calmed me down, 'We can only meet them in safe places where it is difficult for them to draw attention to themselves by attacking us,' he reckoned.

'I am sure that the Smiths' HQ will be surrounded by CCTV cameras. Can you imagine how unpopular they would be if they caused an affray outside their paymasters' home?' I enquired as we sped along. 'Why do we need to talk to them anyway?' And the reply was, 'Imagine that you can drag all the different aspects of your quest for revenge, against the system that fundamentally disturbed your life into one clear focus, wouldn't you take that risk?'

Yes, I agreed that to stack up the case by implicating more and more personalities and related situations into my web would help; however, I had to say, 'But we are breaking cover and taking risks far beyond what I intended. And now I'm feeling at a loss to know what are we up to.' He ignored my fears. 'What I suggest we do is position ourselves at the other end of the street, keep the engine running. Make it obvious that if they approach us we will drive off. I will talk to them on my mobile and suggest that we meet them in three days' time in this exact spot I will promise in my most priestly way that we will do our best to have with us Wayne and Winston's package. I will tell them the truth that we don't have it yet but have a good idea where it is.' I wasn't happy.

'Why would they accept this? It all sounds too crazy to me.'

I had great doubts about his plan. 'Do you now think you know where the incriminating stuff is? No you don't do you?'

He wasn't having my negativity. 'At the orphanage from whence they came, where else?'

He was almost smug as he spelled out his master plan. 'The gap of three days will give you the opportunity to summon the press and other authorities to witness the handover of the information and thereby trigger the sensational revelations that you have so long planned for.'

That's how it went. They looked pissed off. It was quite amusing. Your erstwhile comrades went through all sorts of physical distortions. A couple of times I revved the engine even though we were at least a hundred yards away from them. As if on cue two gatekeepers from

Badger Smith's place came outside into the leafy road. The minder quickly got onto his mobile; we could see he was having difficulty explaining what was going on outside the premises.

As Ignatius relayed the three-days bit to Flanagan, he in turn told Mendes, who lifted his hands to heaven and sent a big mime as if to say why? Followed by a 'stick it up you're arse' gesture in our direction. Anyway, they reluctantly agreed. Mendes shook his fist as a warning. The Priest gave the order to leave and I obeyed by reversing at high speed to the end of the road, spun round and headed off. Out of sight we now turned into the side road and quickly parked and ducked down. Moments later we could hear their speeding car zoom past. We had parked ourselves on the other end of the Smiths' estate. It was as if we had disturbed an ants' nest and the soldiers ants were all over the place running this way and that. 'Now we must go back to David and Jennifer's,' said the infallible Priest. 'There is something I must pick up there.' I told him that I must call you and try to explain what a crazy plan we were now involving ourselves in. He agreed. You will, I hope, recall that I left a message on your phone attempting to explain all this.

He revealed that he had left Toby's notes at the house and that we would need them to be able to locate the dead boy's orphanage. Which he thought was named after St Anthony somewhere near Swindon. Can you imagine how I felt? I was in the hands of a compulsive risk taker, something I had trained myself not to be. All the years I had festered in Bourke, New South Wales, biding my time, saving my Australian dollars, listening patiently to the BBC World Service for mentions of my prey's name. Working in the local library I was amongst the first there to use the net. And when Broadband came along I could type in Sutherland's name and follow the bastard. Later on I found David: humble, ever-cautious David Thwaite. Eventually we skyped, after much nudging and mental arm twisting he eventually agreed to record his daily stake-out operations proving he was being used in a pointless exercise and we would try to get Sutherland on tape discussing the stake out, thereby sealing the sting.

Now I find myself racing around London, trying to keep to our deal to expose your mates for the double dealing criminals they so obviously are, while linking my target to yours. A deal I couldn't refuse. If it wasn't for the fact of our mutual arrangement I would have got out of the car and run away from the turbulent Priest. I might as well just go along for the ride. What have I got to lose? Answer: everything. What options do I have? None. A couple of times we thought we were being tailed across town. Ignatius said I was paranoid. I agreed and couldn't think why I shouldn't be.

The next big surprise the inscrutable African pulled out of the hat was to usher Jennifer out of her house and into my car with, 'I think you know each other.' Imagine my shock. What had he told her? My head filled with a new deceit. My brain raced through all the possibilities. She looked aghast. He hadn't told her I was present. 'Hi!' I managed to utter in a voice that wasn't mine. She said nothing but looked as cold as a block of ice. I decided not to bother with, 'Ah, long time, no see.'

'Jennifer had my copy of Toby's notes.'

We sat there in purgatorial silence as he searched for the clue. Finally he said the notes confirmed that indeed it was an orphanage near Swindon and we should waste no time and head off immediately. We travelled only a few yards when Jennifer demanded that we should stop. I glanced back and saw her laser beam eyes focus on the back of Ignatius' head. 'I see no purpose in me continuing on this journey. Particularly in the present company.' I pulled over. She got out. So typically of her, Jennifer closed the door as if it would fly open again if she didn't completely slam it shut. Apart from her shock of seeing me after so many years she kept her wits about her and walked away with dignity. If she had endured the journey she would have at some time had to speak to me and quite possibly would have been put on the spot. As Ignatius already knew the name and rough location of the orphanage, what was he up to, dragging her into one of his Jesuitical tricks?

For a while the journey west went well enough until filling up with petrol we saw them come into the same crowded forecourt some way behind us. We served ourselves as surreptitiously as we could and fled the scene. Had they seen us? 'Do they know where we are going, or, do they know what we know?' we asked each other. As we drove along I tried to call you again. I began to think it unwise to leave messages. Then our clerical brain box came up with the plan for the next twenty-four hours. 'We will go to the central Police station and there I will ask them to help direct me to the orphanage we are looking for. When they ask how come I don't know the location, I will look like a lost foreign Priest and as a favour, redeemable in heaven, ask them to list them for me.'

I pointed out that we could look in the phone book just as well. He thought it a cautious move to use the local police as they will have noted our visit and if anything should happen to us it will be on the record. I think he comes up with these ideas for the hell of it. Also he decided we should go to a second hand van site and purchase a vehicle preferably with some business designs still on the outside. Four hundred hard-earned quid! 'This will disguise us after we pick up the package.'

Irritatingly, it worked. It was a bit of bad luck for Father Ignatius that St Anthony's was a Roman Catholic institution. The nuns flocked round him as if seeking his blessing. He waved his fingers around and I could see his embarrassment. He doesn't like to lie, but was caught out fair and square. Suddenly he changed the subject on them. They wanted to hear about Rwanda and were ready to tut in unison over the sadness of that unforgettable affair. Everything changed when it began to dawn on them that their own prodigal boys were dead. Ignatius dramatized the urgency that we pick up Wayne and Winston's package and take it to the Police in London. St Anthony's was collectively stunned, they clearly had lost some souls whose lives they had valued. We promised to send them full details ASAP. If Ignatius hadn't been a Priest I don't think they would have allowed us to take the five boxes. Having arrived quite recently via road haulage they had been a puzzlement to the Orphanage. Fortunately not knowing what to do with them they had left them in the main hallway. The whole institution turned out to watch us load up and leave.

That night we stayed in a local motel and it was there I came across the investigative journalist Frank Donahue. He had that very day written in the Guardian on the subject of the Home Office's and Customs' use of imported criminals. Spurred on by the current interest in the whereabouts of Leroy Stuart, he went deeper into the mystery. Apparently it's a much wider practice than most people know of. It seems over the years they have imported bad guys from all parts of Africa, Russia, Eastern Europe and the Near East. These informants infiltrate British-based mobs and have led to some successful prosecutions. He asked, how is the public protected? What Donahue wanted to know was what guarantees and promises had their controllers offered the informants and what type of crimes had they committed in their countries of origin. At the end of the long article he drew attention to the case of Delroy Denton. He described his murders of three innocent women and detailed how difficult it had been for the grieving families to wrench acknowledgement of responsibility from the Home Office, it took numerous court hearings to receive any compensation at all. It's clear he asserted that the authorities are reluctant to own up to their involvement and tend to cover up the tracks. On the matter of the Flee Man he asked, where was he now? He described how some months ago he had been released and presumably been sent back to Jamaica to finish his sentence there – but had he? He described how certain unnamed parties had expressed a fear that he 'was out and about' in London's underworld and possibly linked to slaying of Wayne and Winston. He didn't mention the Auntie Yvonne character.

The next morning it was pissing down and we decided I would drive the van and he the hired car. Before we left Ignatius dressed the car as if it was carrying some boxes. This would give the impression that we had the goods if he was spotted. The ever-resourceful Rwandan suggested we meet up at an address in Hackney Wick where he had made friends in the days he was scouting around for Toby. He described them as a completely different set of people to the criminal fellow travellers of the Smith Set. And so they turned out to be. I don't want to name them or give you their contact as they have only been incidental in the game.

On the way back the car must have been spotted by Flanagan and Mendes. I expect they sat all night on a bridge overlooking the M4 waiting for our return. We had agreed not to drive in convoy but to meet up at the motorway service station at Chieveley. As I arrived some twenty minutes later I sensed something was up as soon as I got there. A great commotion had struck the service station. Surrounded by onlookers a fire engine was putting out the charred wreck of our hired car. I waited for twenty minutes or so to see if your two men were there. They weren't. I reckon they had skedaddled, not wanting to meet up with the local fuzz and have to explain themselves. It must have been them. The car looked as if it had been blown up.

I sat there wondering what to do next. I feared for Ignatius' life. That is until I saw a police wagon turn up and go round to the back of the building. I got out of the van and cautiously followed them around. Two officers emerged from the admin office holding tightly onto Ignatius.

'What's he done?' I asked.

'What's it got to do with you?'

'Well, that's my burnt-out car in the forecourt and he was driving it for me. He is a visiting Priest from Rwanda and is here on important business.'

They paused for a second.

'You will be interviewed shortly. Stay by your vehicle.'

'The Priest is with me,' I said, but it didn't stop them.

'As far as we are concerned he hasn't got any papers, could well be an illegal immigrant and quite probably doesn't have a driving licence. He was reported behaving in a disturbing manner. So I suggest that you wait here until you're called.'

I was lucky not to be detained as an accessory there and then. Ignatius could see the danger: 'You go ahead and please call Jennifer and tell her of my plight.' That was the last I saw of him.

It was on the eve of the General Election that I began to sort out the boxes in the video editing studio, previously hired by Ignatius in an old Hackney Wick warehouse.

You might recall that the proposed meeting with Mendes and Flanagan was scheduled for the actual Election Day 6th May. Neither Ignatius or myself had connected the two dates together. I left you a message, text and voice, saying I hadn't contacted the press as yet and without the Priest to accompany me I felt it was too much of a risk to go to the rendezvous on my own. I bet by then they would be frantic. Having heard from neither of us how could they be sure that they had destroyed the files in the car?

I called Jennifer to tell her what had happened. She just about spoke to me, her words were dragged out through a tight lipped mangle.

'Two thoroughly dislikeable policemen accused me of wasting police time.'

Oblivious of her connections they actually threatened her if she didn't finger us.

'Squaring the circle,' I quipped. She didn't respond, just put down the phone, called me straight back and asked for the details of Ignatius' arrest. I asked her not to give out my number. She put down the phone again. I suppose I was now in her hands again.

The tapes are numerous and centred round the easily recognizable boss. At first I watched a container marked 'Smith Family Holidays. Jamaica. Czech, Slovenia, Moldova and Columbia'. Later on I noticed that Badger's 'Charities' often showed up at the same location as did a box of 'Business Meetings'.

All this stuff is shot in a casual manner, unobtrusive

recordings. The lads certainly had the confidence of the Smiths. Most of the material has a complimentary electronic soundtrack inserted in the editing at a later date. At the bottom of one box I found an edited amalgamation of the above recordings and papers, plus the holiday shots, which linked up the two files. This material also has a complimentary electronic soundtrack that occasionally incorporates the ambient sounds – for instance, at a rural printing press in Slovenia, close to a Czech city, where great fun was had by the family jumping back and forth across the border line. The editing of this event suggests that a serious meeting was disguised as a charity event with the Family Smith draped around various goings on. In Chisinau Moldova we see and hear Wayne and Winston with Badger himself, eyeing up the beautiful young women, taking long shots of smartly dressed teenagers, the lads had contrasted the voyeuristic banter with some falsely enthusiastic girls lounging around in a neon-lit basement in what looks like a London health spa.

Rarely the material gets close to recording actual conversations. It's shot in the middle distance with its unspecific sound track. Obviously Wayne and Winston weren't expected to do anything else but record outings and family highlights.

It slowly dawned on me that the clever little rascals were making a documentary. Shot on two cameras the edited tapes juxtapose the family wealth with the arrivals and departure of all sorts of intermediaries and go-fors doing their daily bidding. Exercising their considerable power it's made clear that the Smiths rule OK.

Another theme was St Anthony. Somehow the saint of desert wanderings who made his name confronting demons pops up all over the place, sometimes with Badger presenting gifts, even cheques to pious-looking functionaries. In the middle of the edited material the Wiltshire orphanage is suddenly featured. The same nuns we met are seen fussing around the Badger. Presumably it's the boys behind the lens. Smith must have felt safe, as these loyal recruits originally came from St Anthony's orphanage of which he is the patron.

We see a montage of clips featuring Britain's number one criminal family with all sorts of European Christians, Coptics from North Africa, various types of Muslims, Jews, Black Pastors and group of holy men in suits watching what I reckon might be a Zoroastrian fire dance.

A balding man in horn rim glasses regularly features, always smiling in the background, even waves at us once. Suddenly we cut to a rare close up of the Badger and Baldy, and as the camera pulls back, lo and behold they're shaking hands outside the Bank of Tbilisi. Badger is ushered in, in VIP mode with a welcoming committee of smiling employees clapping his entrance.

What it all means I can't fathom. I can imagine if serious charges were brought against the Smith family syndicates and their underworld of dodgy dealings, these edited shots could be used to backup the hard evidence illustrating the reach of their crime web. Is this what the boys were intending or were they collecting evidence that somehow they thought would protect them if their positions were challenged? I can't tell what their motives were but the edited material tells a fascinating story.

They certainly get around. Often it's the whole family handling ancient artifacts, holding them up as trophies for the patient cameras. In one long tape and dressed as if on safari the Smiths enthuse over an Ethiopian monastery. As if on cue Badger steps forward with local dignitaries and benignly smiling Government Minister-types pose for the camera. The clearly admired generous benefactor nods to himself, as if to acknowledging his own goodness, hands over a cheque. Later that night a totally different mood emerges as the intoxicated Londoners wine and dine on the fat of the land dressed in expensive native garb. The still suited government flunkies pretend to relax and enjoy the raucous party. Eventually there is a toast and embrace between the locals and the Badger. We can only assume that the deal's done, the looks of trust between them tell us whatever it is – it is an important moment. This piece ends with a close up of a newspaper headline, 'BADGER'S DESERT VISION'.

In a Paris auction house we see the man from the Bank holding a phone whist bidding for a medieval box. The hammer comes down and success is relayed via the phone. It turns out that the old box contains the remains of the gangsters' patron saint. Back at the London compound, guests are blindfolded and ask to shake the box and guess its contents. No one gets its right. All have to feign enthusiasm when they're finally told.

It never becomes clear what the old man gets out of his St Anthony obsession. I think it is something to give him kudos, a distraction from his real business of being the banker for organized crime. At one time he is seen handing over yet another cheque to St Antony's College, Oxford, this time mixing with an array of foreign professors. Interviewed on telly outside the ancient walls we hear him talking about international trade and his fascination with the Egyptian mystique. Who could accuse him of being anything other than a lay collector and kind old benefactor? Except it's common knowledge he's a crook, but it seems few are prepared to tell him to his face.

A sinewy, oldish black woman appears with Mendes and Flanagan outside St Anthony's Church in Hackney. A camera on a tripod is left running and Wayne and Winston join the pose. This must be Auntie Yvonne, she is obviously respected by the four young men, who carry boxes into the church and in front of the camera compete to please her.

In 2009 Mendes and Flanagan begin to regularly show up, showing off in the Smiths' pool, guests at barbeques etc. Our filmmakers concentrate a lot of footage on the two friendly cops, never in close up but always panning over to include them.

Then suddenly we are up to date. Wayne or Winston on camera are distinctly seen, and heard threatening your erstwhile mates.

'If you don't fucking leave us alone we will show Badger the film of you nicking his gear.'

'That would be your death warrant signed, sealed and fucking delivered by me,' retorts Flanagan.

The cops are seemingly unaware of the concealed cameras. The physically bruised Wayne and Winston are seen desperately brandishing a shotgun and a pistol, pointing them in all seriousness at their foe.

'We are out and gone. You can tell anyone you want to tell that if any fucker comes near us we will shoot them. You're included. So fuck off now. Now! Now out.'

They do just that backing out pointing fingers. Flanagan mimes a throat being cut. The last video shots are of the subdued boys, filming each other sniffing large lines of cocaine and spliffing in a flat, armed and resigned. It's like they're waiting for their fate. Having read both Toby's and Ignatius' notes I feel sure this is the top floor flat in Hackney Wick where they eventually made their last stand.

So what to do with all this stuff, which to remind you of the obvious, is not why I am here, ensconced as I am in the bohemian enclave of Hackney Wick? Apart from your cryptic text informing me that you are monitoring the situation, I am in the dark waiting further instruction as per agreement.

You could describe Ignatius' contacts as an open-minded lot, mostly being involved in the arts. Or shit like that. It surprised me that on Election day how many of them voted, taking the whole process seriously. Mainly Labour, some Greens and first time voters choosing Liberal Democrats, no one owned up to voting Tory, although I bet most of their parents residing in the Shires did.

Against the national trend Central London stayed Labour, even the unpopular and devious Hackney Council benefited and increased its majority in the local election held on the same day. It seems the Capital feared the promised swingeing Tory cuts, as if they will stop them. In his Surrey constituency Sutherland was also returned with an increased majority.

At first there was joy in this neighbourhood as it became clear that the Tories failed to win an outright majority in the country at large, having been flagged up for months in the press as dead cert winners. To almost everyone's astonishment the supposedly progressive Liberal Democrats chose to join in a coalition with their historic enemy, this took everybody by surprise and dashed my hopes that Sutherland would become Tory Home Secretary.

My whole plan of nailing the fucker has been predicated on the certainty of an outright Tory victory. I fear now that my exposé won't mean as much. Sutherland could use the system for years, despite being in the opposition to the ruling Labour Government, and with his cross-bench position manipulate the division to his advantage.

Despite this set back it is still a good story isn't it? I can still prove that he used his praetorian class privileges, to sanction nefarious practices that suited himself. There he was confidently waiting in the wings for the new Government's call to high office. He didn't even get a minor Home Office post. Despite my disappointment at his failure to be promoted centre stage, I still promise you he will fall on his sword by the time I'm done with him, even if I have to push him onto it. Unfortunately the public execution I for so long spent my waking days planning won't be so spectacular and might take more time to come to fruition. A time bomb waiting for the right moment to explode.

As I plan soon to leave dear old Blighty, old-school right-wing Conservatives are either hiding in the hills or pretending on telly to be happy that their expected Government posts have – hey presto! – been taken by another rival party now in a Coalition arrangement. In between the days and nights I have spent scouring the Wayne and Winston tapes I've kept one eye open for comments from a chaste Sutherland; but not a word. He will still be there, though, exercising his shadowy power, pulling the strings, serving his masters as well as himself; you can bet on that. Britain is about to change, claim the new Coalition of emboldened public school boys, who while fascinating the fawning media, find themselves, they claim, in the middle of a financially challenged nation.

Volcanic ash blowing over from Iceland managed to close the airports for days; while the airline unions despite a huge majority, have had to appeal to the High Court three times to win permission to go on strike and withdraw their labour. It seems that they had failed to tell the press that eleven ballot papers were spoilt in the process. The nice people around me consider that the cabin staff who want to protect their hard-won rights are asking too much.

'We're all expecting cuts as the hard times set in,' is a common sentiment. 'We all will need to buckle under.'

You can't ask why and get a coherent answer. Why would them losing out on their working conditions help save the nation? Trade unions and workers' solidarity along with it seems to have evaporated. The organized are widely seen a selfish. I point out the bankers got rich and the compliant Labour Government bailed them out and now the poor are expected to pay the cost. People agree that it's all wrong but since I last was here, with a few exceptions, the population seem to accept the twists and turns of a runaway neo-liberal capitalist economy as a fact of life. There is a sort of inverted sadism in the way the man in the street accepts that there are going to be inevitable cuts, as if the harsh economic punishment will be good for them.

Way back when I left the country the Establishment was held in suspicion and the media was a source of lies and deceit especially amongst the young. I was shocked in the cinema recently to witness the audience actually enjoying the smug ads, clapping at the aren't we clever Orange mobile phone commercial. We used to jeer at pretentious ads take the piss out of the 'good-looking' models, think of a witty jibe to shout out. Nowadays it seems, even serious newspapers carry celebrity trivia.

One-time alternative comedians now advertise Banks. The horrors of an expensive Nuclear Power future, once resisted, now is accepted. Before this election Liberal Democrats stood against the costly Trident Missile but suddenly they don't. Entrenched poverty exists as education focuses on the privileged; it was ever thus, but now it's accepted as inevitable.

The incoming Liberal Democrat Deputy Prime Minister declared the other day the biggest reform bill since 1832, catching up with the antipodean electoral system and a welcome turn away from centralized surveillance. Which made me laugh. There was little excitement in Hackney Wick at this news. Will these long-overdue voting reforms help? They might. What's so obvious is that little will be done to alter the ingrained class system which is so set in stone, accepted as the way of things, in place for ever.

The acceptance of the way things are, is illustrated by the nearby Olympics investment. The phlegmatic Brits just accept that it's going to happen whether they like it or not, it cost each and every one of them a lot in taxes. Apparently the inhabitants of the nearby London Boroughs were at first promised all sorts of community involvement. They bemused locals stoically told me that they didn't believe anything much would actually happen and sure enough due to the predictable cost-saving exercises blah, blah, blah, it turns out it won't. Little will spill over to engage the locals.

Some lucky ones are being asked to volunteer to work for nothing to help run the multi-billion-pound extravaganza. I can image the bemused docile population experiencing the delights of imported stilt walkers passing through the streets advertising the proximity of the games; which most will watch on telly for two weeks along with the rest of the world despite living in Hackney Wick next door to the fuss.

So confident that only a few will say, 'Hang on a minute what's this all about?' international entertainment conglomerates are bidding to purchase the public-financed stadiums. They openly plan to privatize them as soon as the games are over. Just as the financiers have taken over the country's assets, so will it be seen as 'sensible' for them to pocket these trinkets. My experience is that few know how and where to complain and most seem to think that the pace of rip-off is inevitable. Tony Blair ignored the last great protest, hundreds of thousands have died in his wars since. I fear the British tradition of resistance has finally chucked it in. Those who can read will cling to their iPads while the in shadows increasingly ignorant millions who can't read or write will watch as educated foreigners do the low paid jobs. I bet Badger Smith is sniffing out the possibilities.

I rang Jennifer, she did not answer. I didn't leave a message. I stuffed the tapes in the back of the van and covered them with old paint cans. I put the vehicle on a single yellow line behind the new multi-million-pound Hackney Town Hall. I returned in half an hour and it had gone, somewhere safe I hoped.

I tried you again, then I texted you my moves. Here are mine. I writing this on the plane somewhere over Europe.

I climbed over backyard fences until I reached Jennifer's

house. She was in her living room stretched out on a chaise longue and listening to music on an old-fashioned pair of earphones. I watched her for a while, she lay still, absorbed in whatever she was tuned in to. I crept round to the front to see if I could spot a stake out. There was nothing obvious. I went to the backdoor and knocked.

'Who's there?' she challenged.

I found it hard to reply, 'It's me… Al.'

'Oh. I was expecting you.'

She unbolted the door, stood there and stared, 'Well'. If you ever meet her you would know how one of her 'Well's' could unsettle the most self-confident man. I gathered myself together and asked, 'Any news about Ignatius?' I felt like an errant schoolboy. Can so-and-so come out and play?

She decided to invite me in. As I started to speak, she held her finger to her lips, ushered me into the downstairs bathroom. Closing the door Jennifer turned on two sink taps and ran the shower. She even flushed the loo. Now confident we could speak without being heard we both laughed an unfriendly restrained laugh. She whispered, 'I have been in touch with him, he is being held in Paddington Green Police Station. Apparently his papers pass muster. I was told they're interested in a burnt-out car in a motorway service station.'

'Who told you?' I dared to ask.

'Who do you think you pious prick?'

'The main man in your life.'

She slapped my face, then apologized and then asked me what I wanted.

Nigel, I have to tell you that in this close confinement I wanted her. All these years later I still fancy her to bits. This will sound yucky but there is a chemistry between her and me. Honestly, I pushed it out of my mind. She did what she first did when I first ever met her. She surprised me as she stretched her hand out and fondled my cock. I probably couldn't resist that if anyone I half liked did that. But Jennifer touching me almost brought tears to my eyes.

Well, the rest of it is not anybody else's business. Physically we are so compatible. We lay in bed and talked. So much was revealed to me. It was strange because I could appreciate that she had learnt a lot as a counsellor. She listened and occasionally asked a leading question yet every now and again we would become intimate, as if there was so much for us both to catch up on. I was still there way into the morning.

I told her as if she was now my counsellor, about my consuming hatred of Malcolm Sutherland, how I had eventually fled to the 'Back of Bourke' a pleasant enough town in New South Wales, where for more than a few years I had festered in the Australian outback, a fish out of water, an inner whingeing Pom. Sitting on the banks of the muddy Darling River I would cry with frustration, eventually forcing myself to become positive and plan a long-term scheme of revenge. I think it was Confucius who said 'If you wait long enough by the river bank the body of your enemy will float past.'

I explained how relatively recently I had made contact with David. She just listened as I told her that he felt used by her and the MP. I explained it was my idea to bug his and Patricia's conversations as a way to prove that both of them were unaware they were being used, and that their stake-out duty was a ploy to keep him out of the house. Her house for fuck's sake! At that point she just indicated that I should tell my version.

I wanted Sutherland to be shown as a two-timing manipulator. I could feel that she could understand my thirst for revenge. Incongruously I was lying in bed beside her telling her all this. It didn't seem to disturb her professionalism that she was the subject of my sting. I could feel her twinge when I mentioned Patricia but other than that I felt free to continue. She nodded when my account of the tale coincided with her recollection of hearing Patricia's anxiety about this Auntie Yvonne murder and the unwelcome involvement of your team in the tale, how deep it went as Britain's Number One criminal institution the Badger Smith outfit joined the link.

I told her of your approach to me, about the Wayne and Winston's slaughter and the fear of the return of the licensed murderer Leroy Flee Man Stuart. How Ignatius joined with me but seemed to want to protect her. Although the whole thing had got out of hand it and it was a long way from my first intention to suggest that Sutherland and her were having it off while David was at a stake out daily on a wild goose chase. Nevertheless it would stick. I believe the press would love it. True or not the truth never concerned them. Where there is mud there could be a mire. I said straight out that I didn't think that she and he were intimate. She was a bit surprised when I told her the pictures I have taken of him arriving and the both of them going off together in his chauffeur driven car.

Toby had open up my story. Whether it's true or not didn't matter to me, as long as it stuck. I could link three undercover Home Office sanctioned cops to the Smiths, royalty, drugs, police protection of institutionalized crime, murders and murderers, corruption, and the old Establishment practice of being beyond the law, protecting their class interests as they felt the need to do so. I can link them all back to my arch enemy, the man who had me pissed on so to gain a foothold.

By this time Jennifer had turned a bit cold as the full weight of possibilities dawned on her. Her professional mask slipped a bit. She began to talk in a considered way and I began to learn and listen. She had never wanted to see me dragged off to detention. She admitted that life with her husband was dull. In a low tone she described how it was that once they were in the Police web they couldn't become unstuck.

There were always new things, semi-state secrets that others didn't have. They found it hard to mix with ordinary folk. She had tried hard to make it work with David, agreed to the mortgage, had the twins taken up counselling.

Suddenly she sat up and told me the astonishing fact,

that the link with Sutherland was far from what I had speculated. As if making an important decision she turned to me and confirmed that.

'I counsel those who have been involved in torture,' Jennifer became bright eyed.

'You might as well know that any hope of splashing stories across the media would be doomed to failure as it would be censored. We all know that Britain doesn't own up to involvement in rendition. What we don't know is that they actually do the interrogations themselves.' I shouldn't have been surprised after all they had done it to me. All that stuff about Her Majesty's Government cannot condone torture is of course bollocks. But how naïve I have been. I hadn't suspected that they were into actually doing it for themselves. How could they trust anyone but themselves? How dumb is that? Jennifer's job is to deal with the casualties, if that's the best way to describe the perpetuators. She sees those who have become mentally disturbed by the cruelty they've done to their fellow human beings.

'There is no way they are going to let that out into the public domain.' Her old self-assured arrogance had returned.

'I thought torturers did it because it turned them on.'

'No, not all, many find themselves sliding into it. The boundaries of what's acceptable and what is not aren't clear. The rewards of breaking someone can lead to promotion. You join an inner circle. Some can't continue they need help. What they have done is after all illegal and the State denies it takes place. There aren't that many who crack up. They send them to me. Its top secret, David doesn't know.'

'But now you've told me.'

'Yes but even if you shout it from the roof tops nobody will be able to report it.'

'Does Toby or the Priest know?'

'No.'

'Why me?'

'Because if you spread your tales about Sutherland, the runaway cops, dead Auntie Yvonne, Home Office murderers, the Smiths and Uncle Tom Cobbleigh and all, I think they will move against you. You might well see yourself holding up one of the Olympic concrete pillars forever.'

'I'm leaving for Bourke on the next flight I can get.'

I teased her: 'Toby will be waiting for me there,' I wanted to hurt her.

'And when Ignatius is free I expect he will join us.'

She suddenly looked lonely. 'Why don't you join us?'

'Who knows I might even do just that.'

We lay there for a while rediscovering our physical compatibility. She seemed to want me to stay. Eventually David came home. I guess Jennifer expected him. He called out, she answered him. I didn't know what to do. He came into the bedroom.

'You cunt!' he exploded.

'Which one?' Jennifer queried.

'Both of you!' he cried and slammed the door so hard that ornaments fell off the shelves.

7. Open Letter from Detective Nigel Onobolu

TO WHOM IT MAY CONCERN

I got my marching orders on 16th June 2010, the day after the new Prime Minister accepted Governmental responsibility for the 1972 Bloody Sunday Derry Massacre and on the same day as the death of Malcolm Sutherland MP.

On reading the news the first thing I thought of as I travelled into my hastily summoned meeting with my superior officers, was the sudden irony of my links to the dead MP, the troubles in Ireland, Aloysius O'Connor's revenge obsessions and my ongoing investigation into the Smith syndicate. If the link is Ireland, it's certainly something I have had absolutely nothing to do with in all my forty-four years.

The papers talked of closure and suggested in their self-righteous style that the atrocities committed by the Parachute regiment all those years ago would best be left on the shelf. O'Connor for his part had left the scene of his crime hoping that someone else would take his research down from the proverbial shelf and pass it around. I do feel like getting my own back. I too would like to throw some shit.

The Daily Telegraph obituary noted that Malcolm Sutherland MP had served a number of times on a parliamentary committee concerned with the bitter struggle in the troubled Irish Province. He will be remembered 'As an authority on the subject of National Security.'

It will annoy O'Connor that his enemy's suicide wasn't as much of a big media deal as he would have hoped. The 'Tragic loss' was mainly eclipsed by breaking news of oil leaks in the Gulf of Mexico, the immanent retreat of the euro-zone economies, plus the incoming Coalition Government's austerity Budget, not forgetting England's dismal showing at the South African World Cup.

Very little was made of the method of his death, hanging from a beam in his Wraysbury mansion. Most surprising was the speed of the 'foul play is not suspected' news release rushed out before any real investigation could have taken place.

The Prime Minister's statement received cross-party support from the House of Commons, for the 'unswerving commitment Sutherland had unstintingly given to the Nations interests.' 'Hear, hear', they all agreed on the 'sad' news.

A Sunday Times columnist hinted that Sutherland was deeply disappointed that he hadn't been included in the new Government: that was it, not much more then that. I don't believe in conspiracy theories, never have, but when everything comes on at once it's difficult not to put two and two together and come up with a mathematical puzzle too complex to comprehend.

In the matter-of-fact interview that day I had with my superior officers, some I knew, some I didn't, I was a given a nine-month sabbatical. 'We want you to stand down from what has become a 'political issue.' Go away somewhere, aren't you of Nigerian extraction? Why don't you visit your homeland? See the sights, so to speak.'

I just about managed to ask, 'What of my two fellow officers Flanagan and Mendes?'

They looked at each other and after a nod or two managed to squeeze out, 'They have volunteered to serve as advisors to the Afghanistan Police.' Before I could even think to ask they promptly added, 'There was only a call for two to go.' That was it. Nothing was said about when or how I should return. Only later did I find I was on basic pay guaranteed for six months. I sat in my room for a few days, maybe a week, as the news sank in. Had I been too keen? Ruffled feathers? Trod on toes? Discovered something I wasn't supposed to discover? That was it – saving what I have read in The White Van Papers as I have come to refer to them. From Aloysius O'Connor, bugging set up with David Thwaite, how that expediently led to the knowledge of Auntie Yvonne's funeral, the Smiths, the Flee Man, Wayne and Winston's murder, Jennifer Thwaite's involvement with psychologically disturbed torturers and the too-coincidental death – the meat in the middle of the sandwich – of the late Malcolm Sutherland MP. Al O'Connor once remarked, 'If you want to put a bit of shit in the context of society you'd have to look at the whole sewer.'

My problem is that I once believed in what I was doing. I got it from my parents. We lived in Guildford. At the

Poly I was teased as 'British Nigel', the joke being that I dressed in English styles, played cricket and with my parents attended Matins at Guildford Cathedral – both were keen members of the C of E congregation. My dad is so proud that during the war he made sergeant in the RAF, my mum a nurse. We thought racism was for other people. Unlike the Nigerians who came later, we weren't happy-clappy born-again evangelicals, conniving accountants or alienated traffic wardens. We were old school Empire and believed in British fair play and justice. My parents were overjoyed when I joined the Police to serve my country.

Over the years I found it hard to tell them of my undercover work and the duplicity involved in my relationship with the twilight criminal world. They put it down to professional secrecy. That will do.

I contacted one of our family friends, Sheila Yashere – both sets of parents had hoped that we would eventually marry each other. I kept her secret, she was gay and she knew she owed me. Sheila is very bright, worked her way up in the Home Office. She was surprised that I called her.

'Is it Christmas already?'

'I need to see you.'

'Isn't once a year enough?'

'Have you ever been to the RIBA café in Portland Place?'

That did it. She can't miss a chance of gaining a brownie

point. We met the next day. I decided not to tell her too much, pretend that I was still on active service. I invented a ruse, I was in an unofficial departmental competition to find out as much as I can about Leroy Stuart 'the Flee Man' and if I did I would get noticed by my bosses.

'It could lead to promotion and who knows what?' I lied. She bought it. Didn't even query how come the info couldn't be accessed through normal channels. She just accepted that the system doesn't always work.

'All I want to know is where he is now, so that we can keep our records straight. It's become a puzzle to us all. I thought of you. I didn't let on I knew you. I'll keep it a secret.'

Sheila loved secrecy and promised she would get to the bottom of the mystery as long as I never let on it was her. Little did I know the files she opened would lead to her instant dismissal a month later. Three days after our meeting she called and we agreed to meet in the middle of Hyde Park.

'What I've done for you, phew! There was all sorts of blocks put on his case. What a thoroughly nasty man. It's as if his file has been opened and ordered to be closed by so many different departments. It took me hours to claw my way though. No wonder your lot found it difficult. I don't know what the fuss is all about. It's a cut and dried case. He has been dead for a couple of months. It seems that as his wishful thinking request for parole came up he was immediately bundled off back to Jamaica.

'It was soon realized that this backdoor deportation was open to legal objection and had to be returned here It seems there were outstanding matters, Habeas Corpus and others. He arrived back stone cold dead. Apparently the authorities in Kingston put him in a cell with his arch enemies. He was dead within twenty four hours. I passed over the details of his execution; they were long and detailed and I imagine extremely awful.'

I didn't let on what a bombshell this was to me. She wanted to leave.

'Don't ask me to do this again. Clearly the whole case has been a mess for years and I don't think the Home Office want these sorts of dealings made public. So keep me out of it.' She left in a bit of a huff. There had been a feeling of foreboding in her voice. I still have to seek her forgiveness.

Over the years the feeling that I was doing something useful has evaporated, drop by drop. My belief in the ultimate pragmatic progressive goodness of our system dried up. I've got by taking an interest in whatever the task is I find myself involved in; as it was with the Smiths. As I saw it, our task was to use the connection to the Port Royal Night Club and make it work both ways. The protection we three 'black fellows' offered to the minor Monarchical ravers provided us with cover to sus out the Smith drug deals. We were briefed to take our time: 'Don't frighten the horses'. To the Smiths we were protecting the Royals as they crossed the tracks and did a bit of "slumming" and to the Hooray Henrys and their upper class followers we posed as the real thing. Street wise, black and very friendly. Whatever went down, at no cost, we were instructed, 'The press must not get to hear about it.' If all we had been required to do was to be chaperones then I wouldn't have bought it. I find it hard to be pleasant at the best of times. The Smiths became my personal target. I could see the institutional evil they represented, parasitical ciphers off the commonwealth in a slowly rotting society. Bent bankers, wholesalers off the back of a lorry, easy money, merchants of deceit, they became a suitable target for my energy.

A week passed. I wasn't expecting any news. I found it difficult to know what to do next. And I wanted to do something. On the seventh day I received two calls in a matter of hours. I didn't pick up either. The priest Father Ignatius left his name and number and hung up. The second call was from the Badger.

'We should meet. Can you suggest somewhere? Cheers.'

It was to become a habit. I left a message on Badger's personal number.

'How about the RIBA café Portland Place, next Tuesday, 11 a.m.?'

I rang Ignatius' number, asked him to meet at my ground-floor flat in Somers Town. I figured he would trust me more if I invited him to where I live. He was with me within an hour.

I had last met him in the flat of the slain boys in Hackney Wick, now we were meeting in a different atmosphere. Stiff with each other at first I could see he was having difficulty relaxing. After second thoughts he would have a brandy. I brought him up to date. As Al O'Connor had noted, his priestly vibe gives one confidence to confide in him. I confessed to him; I hadn't told anyone else my news.

'I have been given the push from the Met. I am at a lost about what to do next.'

He took on an old-fashioned air of a sleuth. I told him about the death of Leroy the Flee Man Stuart. He even gasped at the details and noted the facts in his little book.

'So he didn't kill the lads?' It was more a statement of the obvious then a question.

'No, or Auntie Yvonne.'

'Does pushed mean dismissed?'

'I expect it will do. Certainly will if I get further involved, now I am suspended.'

'Pushed off the case but still paid?'

'Yes.'

'You are in more danger if you carry on. Yet I think you will carry on. As the English like to say, "You can't let the bastards grind you down", can you?'

'No…I hear you were locked up in the Edgware Road anti-terrorist cells. How easy was that?'

'Not easy at all. I saw the funny side when two of my gaolers tried "to get my goat". They blasphemed Jesus making sexual references about him sucking their cocks. Why doesn't he come to help me? They were surprised when Jennifer did. I knew my papers were in order. They had to let me go.'

'Didn't they question you?'

They weren't interested in the burnt-out hire car; their brief was to see if they could deport me. I was surprised that they hadn't linked the events. If for no other reason it would have given them something to do. Jennifer took me home. She was in a bad state. She told me that David had caught Aloysius and her in bed.'

We changed the subject. He didn't seem to want to talk about the pressure at the Thwaite household. Instead, the Priest stood up and asked as if I knew the answer to his question, 'Who killed Wayne Winston? Was it your one-time comrades Flanagan and Mendes? I think it was. Do You? Yes?'

I gave a professional shrug. He stared at me for a long moment. I felt obliged to fill him in. It was as if a burden lifted from my head. During the last three years I had let it all go in and stay there. Very rarely had I tried to see my daily life in any rational perspective. It had been a rollercoaster of unexpected ups and downs. I basically told myself that I was enjoying the ride. Now unexpectedly it poured out to a Rwandan atheist in priests' clothing, that I wasn't happy at all. It had made me laugh when Patricia Murray labelled us Tom, Dick and Harry. It must have seemed like that to her; but it was far from the truth. The Met had need of undercover cops who fitted their plan, so they welded us together. Mendes and Flanagan knew each other. I had the misfortune to team up with them.

A number of boys had been pushed off tower blocks and the Hackney force had been given the task of gathering intelligence on the deaths. Mendes and Flanagan had been undercover on the vast Council estates. I don't think anybody ever got to the bottom of it. It was a question of 'omerta' as far as the local territorial gangs were concerned. Scotland Yard suspected that the killings were part of the burgeoning crack scene. Well, that was being said officially. I held the theory that it was more likely to be bullying and it was old fashion fear that kept people's mouths shut.

The Met, Customs and Excise, the Home Office and the rest were still embarrassed by their part in the concoction of the Yardie coke fear scandal some years back and needed some element of 'truth' to point to. Crack was beginning ruin lives. I knew police officers who caught the addiction circling the East End looking for gear to confiscate. Coke had become in general use and quality and prices were going down. I once lifted a bag from some yuppies in Shoreditch, it turned out it was something else, it certainly had no effect on us.

The authorities needed to explain just how general drug use was. Lumping coke, crack and pot together they briefed the tabloids. They spent millions chasing their own tails. They had brought the Jamaican psychopathic killers Delroy Denton and Leroy Stuart into the scene to break into what in fact was their own invention. Stuart must have thought he had a licence to kill and was beyond the law – after all, he wasn't officially in the country. Not until he was convicted of the murder of two innocent women did his controllers grudgingly admit responsibility and even then labelled his victims as prostitutes.

Eventually, embarrassed top brass pointed to the Smiths – traditional criminal wholesalers – as a more likely source of the gear but seemed to let it hang. It turned out that Smith had benefited from the Mets' Yardie distraction and obligingly helped finger the Flee Man. It was becoming patently obvious that he was something other than just an agent provocateur. He was endangering all of their collective interests, getting away with it on both sides of the line. It's said that the Badger paid Stuart to kill enemies while he worked for our side; wouldn't surprise me at all. It's now obvious that my one-time partners along with the Smiths and quite probably the Met, have jointly used his recent phantom reappearance as a convenient excuse to…

Ignatius stopped me at this point. 'So you agree it is most likely that Flanagan and Mendes killed Wayne and Winston?' I had to admit it looks that way.

'And Auntie Yvonne? Okay, what I would like to know is, was it done at the Smiths' behalf or were they working alone? How involved were they with the Smiths?'

'It was a part of our double bluff to buy small amounts of class A and B drugs and sell them to the Royals and their retinue,' I explained.

In the inner smug world of the 'in' Met intelligence it's a matter of pride that they are the ones selling drugs to the

Princes' mates and could justify it, if ever questioned, as a sting on the Smiths, as well as safeguarding the young untouchables from the prying media. Badger Smith himself pretended he didn't approve but explained it was his civic duty that through his extensive contacts he knew safe hands that could be trusted to supply safe drugs. That's how the working link came into practice. He added he was proud to help protect the Monarchy and encouraged them to meet at his club without publicity. The quality of the various types of gear was excellent.

I maintain that I was put in charge of our 'excused boots' team because I have a southern counties accent. If we were to be let loose without supervision then for the authorities the class loyalty angle was the strongest bond. That I was a 'chap' and the other two were more 'common', as my Mum would say, gave me authority.

The working truth was that the only way I could lead the unit was by outwitting the others. I came up with targets and debriefings and rotas, as if they had been ordered from above, which mainly they hadn't. The plain fact is that we were there to protect Royals, the rest was pretence. I used the fact that the others were increasingly becoming chummy with the enemy. Their friendship with the Badger Set helped me get to know the main man himself, John Smith. I sense he respected me because I wasn't such an easy knock over as the others. To him I was seen as the main man reporting back to our bosses.

Over some months I let him groom me into 'a working relationship'. While I knew that he knew that I knew he was an out and out villain, it was only ever mentioned between us via wry smiles, sometimes an 'oops' and 'as if ever' shrugs. So it was that I slowly turned a blind eye. I promised myself that in this phoney world, acting as liaison between crime and the State, I would in the end build a case against them both. If I could believe in the honesty of the case, it would justify my duplicity. I never did. I sat on it. The truth is there wasn't any official interest, and that didn't help.

During the Banking Crisis the Smiths released vast amounts of cash into circulation and as a reward were nodded to from on high. A recognition that he had helped with quantitative easing appeared in the Financial Times: *"Unexpected friends help save the cash flow"*. John Smith can be friendly if he likes you, deadly if he doesn't. He takes it as a matter of pride that he can deal with all types of people. He can listen and change his mind as you talk to him. He is a top-quality chief executive officer who I believe blinds himself from the accumulating consequences of his actions. He points to corruption everywhere, yet his morality is based on the notion, just like the economic elite he envies, that he too should be able to help himself to other people's wealth, basically because he can. There is no sense of irony within the man.

Conscientiously, over the months I listed the tentacles of his activities and filed them with the Home Office-sanctioned intelligence unit. During that time I became suspicious of Flanagan and Mendes when we weren't in the Tom, Dick and Harry mode. I discovered they were running errands for minor villains. Both were gaining a dubious reputation in the Roman Road milieu for 'putting in a word' for those charged with minor offences. I devised a roster where we had to hang out together at the Port Royal Club on expenses, keeping eye out for the Royal parties and at the same time monitoring the Smiths. It all started to fall apart at the Auntie Yvonne funeral. The Badger paid for the funeral from his own wallet. She had been useful to both sides of the so-called fence.

She helped the Badger keep people sweet, she boasted she could 'twist his arm' on behalf of local good causes. For the Police she fingered the Vietnamese skunk manufacturers long before heat-seeking helicopters were used. She wasn't respected by Turk or Kurd teams though, having pointed out territorial infringements to the local police as if she was a referee. She was at her happiest with Jamaicans, middle-class English and authority. In her meetings with Hackney Police Inspectors she was in her element reporting on local goings on. Smith asked us to attend her funeral. He said that he had been in contact with our bosses and had agreed with them that it was in the interest of all the concerned parties to keep the event out of the press and any other prying interests.

Ignatius listened to my confessional debrief, taking notes with great patience. 'Thus the "circle is squared",' he suddenly pronounced. 'When PC Patricia Murray hears on the local grapevine that Auntie Yvonne is about to be buried in Kensal Rise Cemetery she gets there late and unbeknown to her the effect of her unexpected arrival is that the two worlds – how do you say? – enter each other.'

'Go on, then,' I encouraged.

'DC Murray is unaware that she been fitted into the stake-out car as a make weight to David Thwaite who has been bargained to keep him in work and out of the way, while his wife is on a hush-hush task supervising treatment for disturbed torturers, who don't officially exist. I contend that she is a supervisor in a chain of physiological processes that deal with the State's own in-house casualties. The best way the whole plan could be hidden is by a network of 'normal' practices that assess and treat patients who are under orders to deny what they've been up to.'

His intense brainstorm suddenly came to an abrupt end. Ignatius asked, 'Where exactly is the van now?'

We rushed to the Hackney Pound, which turned out wasn't in Hackney. The Nigerian supervisor accepted the UN official undercover story from a Nigerian-looking detective and the imprimatur of a holy Rwandan. Yet, this son of the Empire felt free to drag us through as much form filling as he could throw at us. If they still had rubber stamps to stamp it would have made his day. We were lucky. A fully road taxed, builders' van from Swindon had been reprieved from an 'unclaimed' crushing, as it been considered that it might have been of police interest, and here we were claiming it, backed up by Aloysius' purchase receipt.

I had found the address of the Guardian journalist Frank Donahue. He lived in a leafy lane in Chingford, and I suggested that Ignatius drive the van over there and park it as near as he could to where the man lived on a free-parking street. We sat for what seemed like hours as the process worked itself out. The van was blocked in the back lot and an extra hand was needed to come on shift to shunt it round to the front.

It wouldn't have been such a big deal if Aloysius hadn't agreed with David Thwaite that they would both take out their separate revenge on Sutherland; but 'come to think of it' they needed each other. It was a clever idea to counterattack the system by bugging chit-chat to prove corruption. Giving David something 'to do' is the time honoured practice in dealing with the cuckold, even though it's not sex in this case. Sometimes maybe it was!

Ignatius concluded with the pronouncement, 'She needs him for protection. She always has. Always found him things to do over the years, always setting the agenda. He has come to resent it.'

The Priest was excited he was at last undoing a difficult knot. As he stood up to go and sign the final release form I noticed how shabby his garb was. His clerical collar had lost its whiteness, his jacket was frayed, unwinding at the sleeves. I wondered what his next set of clothing would be. When he has funds will he buy more clerical gear?

The next time I met Ignatius was at his request at McGinty's Goat in Kilburn. He wolfed down their biggest steak.

'This is where they bugged Malcolm Sutherland and the shit hit the fan.'

He took precious time from his meal to tell me.

'Just by meeting again we were sealing the deal. Whatever it was we were about to do we have joined forces and have a common enemy.'

We never really had agreed long-term tactics or objectives and I'm not sure it's the way I like to work but still it reassured him.

'I will write to Frank Donahue the journalist and tell him where to find the van key. I'll suggest the links are up to him to make whatever he can of them.'

He nodded.

'In a way,' I said, 'it's a pity that Malcolm Sutherland is dead.'

'He wasn't when we went to see him; but he was soon after.'

'Who, you're kidding …. Who went?'

'Jennifer and myself, didn't you know?'

'Of course I didn't know.'

'Well, I thought I'd better "let you in on it", as they say. Now that we are "partners in crime".'

'Yes, I think so. What happened?'

'Jennifer told him about Aloysius' bug. He got very cross with her and they shouted at each other. She pointed out that he must not have been reading his briefings as the Australian secret service was hand in glove with British and American intelligence. He could have kept tabs on O'Connor. He said that she was off her rocker. She said she had from time to time been kept informed. She knew that Aloysius O'Connor was in Bourke. He was dumbfounded. He became annoyed with her pointing out over the years how he had looked out for them finding roles for David – 'That ungrateful drone', he called him. Jennifer counterattacked screaming that she had served him well over the years and had filled in for his lack of human credibility. He said if it wasn't for him she wouldn't be where she was today. She agreed – 'compromised'. Then she 'spelt it out' as you say.

'Your new Conservative and Liberal Coalition Government will do all it can to distance itself from Blair's wars. It is a good and handy way of damaging the previous Labour Government reputation and washing their hand of their years of compliance.' Sutherland listened while she 'dotted the I's and crossed the T's'.

Most people in Britain were against the Iraq war by the end and are now beginning to hear that the Taliban are winning a guerrilla war in Afghanistan. The Labour leadership tried to censor Britain's involvement in the CIA rendition process, but despite their effort it sneaked out. Just wait till it comes out that they were doing it themselves. Ignatius spelt it out.

'The MP went ashen as he added up the possibilities. He quietened down and asked Jennifer what he should do.

'Jump the gun,' she counselled.

'Come clean before they get to you. You could say that

you were shocked to find out what was going on. How you set up help for the victims and their over-enthusiastic inquisitors but were blocked by the Cabinet.'

The shaken MP had suddenly sat down.

'You can claim you protested at what was going on.'

She waved her hand at him and the Priest said he saw her in a new light as she then made the crucial point.

'Your side won't defend you, nor will any of Secret Service departments once it gets out. And it will.'

We left. The next day he was dead by his own hand I believe. The hungry Priest downed two puddings, a coffee and a brandy. Eventually we both left together. Outside we went our separate ways.

****

John 'Badger' Smith was already in the architects' cafeteria, when I arrived, a minder was sitting some tables away.

'Well, young man, I certainly can say that I don't turn on to this… décor.'

'"Utilitarian" it says on the website.'

He waved it all away at my reply. It was like he wanted to be my friend, sort of chatty even. 'No it's not for me. My wife says I haven't advanced beyond mock Tudor. I can do neo-gothic if I have to. But this… this makes me feel intimidated. I am most at home in early gothic, round arches and all. Funny isn't it? I was born in Tottenham but over the years my taste is for the ancient world. I can afford it I suppose. I enjoy the idea that one can return to the glories of the past; when things stood for something. When a man's beliefs were his bond before so-called society counted up a man's possessions. We're becoming a nation of accountants.'

I ordered a coffee.

'Thank you for seeing me. I first came here when I was tailing someone.'

Smith put an envelope on the table. I could see it was stuffed with notes.

'This is for you. I heard on the grapevine that you was out of the loop and so were your mates.'

I put the envelope into my inside pocket.

'Thanks.'

'It's ten grand, I gave the same to the others. Anything new you want to talk about? Anything on your mind?'

I needed him to relax. 'How's business?'

'Club's all right, I'm told by my financial advisors to think about getting out of the rented accommodation racket though. Apparently this Coalition Government have got their eyes on rent subsidies. They shouldn't have sold us the Council stock if they didn't want us to make money out of them. They change the game to suit themselves. It's like the fucking Olympics; they gave out the contracts by interview, interview would you believe? Not tender, kept the community investors like me out of it. Just like the World Cup in South Africa only the big multinationals got a look in. Where's the fairness in that? I don't know what this country is coming too. They're all the same, looking after themselves. What's on your mind?'

'Before I left active service a new name popped up a couple of times. I wonder if you have heard of him. He just topped himself.'

'Malcolm Sutherland MP?'

'Yes, how do you know about it?'

'An African Priest asked me the same question only yesterday.'

'A black Priest?'

'Yes, a Father Ignatius, he represents African victims of St Anthony Fire affliction, strangely he didn't mention that fact when I first met him. You know I like people to be straight with me. Do you know him?'

'Did he say he did?'

'No. He told me that the dead MP suffered from the Fire and now you mentioned him.

What's it all about? He had something to do with the Home Office didn't he?'

'Well, the connection is that DC Patricia Murray, who I believe you met due to the Auntie Yvonne mess up, was actually undercover, working out of Sutherland's

Police Committee bag. As you know there was no link between the two.'

'You're not wired are you?'

No, of course not, why?'

'Because I did know him, the Priest was right. We shared a common interest. We both suffer from St Anthony's Fire.'

'Blotchy red skin?'

'It's more complicated than that.'

'Does it hurt?'

'Only when I laugh. Of course it fucking does. I've spent a fortune on it. Some people have it worse than others.'

'Did you meet with Sutherland often?'

'No, at Oxford a couple of times, I don't like Tory toffs at the best of times. What's the point of all this? Come to think of it we were in a documentary together at St Antony's College. Something about Global Economics and the responsibility of the individual, it wasn't for me, not my kind of thing. It's a small world. I have met his minions more frequently since, once they found I had interests in some desert locations, old monasteries et cetera. He put them in touch with me, paid good money for hush-hush secret conferences etcetera, wanted to keep it schtum and I'm their man. If can help the Country I will. The call of duty and all that. What's this got to do with you?'

'The link is that PC Murray and her partner PC David Thwaite were staking out Bob Crow of the RMT...'

'The Communist?'

'They got involved one way or another in Wayne and Winston's deaths.'

'What's that got to do with the Unions?'

'Nothing but because of them Sutherland got to hear about the Flee Man.'

'What, that he is out and about killing people? What's that got to do with him other than the obvious Home Office connection?'

That's when I played my card.'Before he died he told a number of sources that Leroy the Flee Man Stuart had been dead for more than two months, having been killed in a Jamaican prison.'

John Badger Smith got suddenly loud.'What the fuck are you talking about? I'm being set up here!'

'I thought you should know,' I said and got up quickly and left.

'Who told you all this?' he shouted after me.

'My erstwhile bosses,' I lied.

'The fucking cunts!' he bellowed in the busy RIBA café.

Waiting outside my flat reading his notes Father Ignatius was surprised by my frosty attitude.

'How come you went to see John Badger Smith without fucking telling me and mentioning Malcolm Sutherland to him? Al O'Connor warned me about you.'

He had the audacity to blanch at my swearing.

'I went to Mr Smith to seek a donation. I realised that there wasn't going to be much of a chance after you had been to see him. I didn't tell you as I would have "put you off your stride".'

'Are you satisfied?'

'Not really.'

'Did he give you anything?'

'Two hundred in old Scottish pound notes.'

He didn't know whether to look pleased or not. Suddenly there was a thump at the door. We both froze. The door was knocked again, the bell rang, the letter box rattled. I peeped out from the small bathroom window. Outside were the Kiwi twin pugilists, one astride the front door and the other shielding his eyes with his hands to look into my main window.

'Nigel, can you come out and have a word with us? It won't take long,' mocked a New Zealand accent. They knocked again. It felt as if they were going to break in the door. I heard Ignatius leave.

'Sorry, I can't come out and play today,' I shouted back though the letter box.

'Then we will have to come in and play with you won't we!'

I armed myself with a police truncheon and unlocked the door. The twins closed up together.

'We will give you a chance. You fight one of us in a fair fight, or the two of us with one hand tied behind both of our backs or...'

It was too late for them both – the Rwandan came on them from behind wielding my cricket bat. Quickly he smacked both of them in their heads and then hit them hard in their stomachs. Both went down dazed and flat out. I hardly had anything to do with it. Ignatius stood back with the bat above his head, before jumping fiercely on them in turn. 'As they say, "out for six"! I think so.' I took their mobile phones from their jacket pockets and smashed them with my heel. We went back inside, watched them through the window as they eventually roused, helping each other up. In obvious pain they hobbled away bloodied and humiliated. Before they turned the corner one of them turned and waved a revengeful fist.

I gave the Priest another thousand pounds.

'I suggest that you find your way to Bourke and join Toby and Al O'Connor. I expect your friend Jennifer will be there soon enough. Once this shit hits the fan there won't be much for her to do in this country. The combined spooks will be happy that you're all safe tucked up in one place.'

'What will you do?'

He seemed genuinely concerned. I told him that I would write a note to Frank Donahue telling about the van's contents and give him an up to date copy of the stake-out records, so far as Al's notes go.

'Have you considered that David Thwaite might be wagging the dog by the tail? He might have encouraged PC Patricia Murray to attend the funeral knowing that her unexpected attendance would trigger investigation. Or...'

'I don't care about any of that.'

I told the bright-eyed sleuth, 'As long as Smith thinks the Met are setting him up he will go silent. I will, in good time, state that MI6 have been using his desert properties for torture purposes and that once the whistle was blown; Sutherland killed himself. The records show that Mrs Jennifer Thwaite and husband DS David Thwaite have a long record of undercover work on behalf of the State and that she professionally counselled disturbed British torturers. I will assert that the Smiths in all probability colluded with Flanagan and Mendes to kill Wayne and Winston who had made revealing video recordings of them. It will come out that both the Met and Smith knew that their alibi Leroy the Flee Man Stuart was long dead. The question of who killed Wayne Winston will be back on the agenda. It will be too big a story to hide any longer and rival factions in the Met will be tempted to open the books. O'Connor says there is plenty of footage of desert buildings and dodgy people. What made me inwardly cry 'Bingo' was when Smith told me of his meeting with none other than Malcolm Sutherland at St Antony's College, Oxford. I remembered that Al O'Connor describes footage of just such a meeting amongst the lad's video tapes.'

The shit is about to hit the proverbial fan and it's my intention to throw as much in its direction as I can. It took them years to own up to the Derry slaughter and I've looked it up, its official they water-tortured prisoners in the Troubles in the North of Ireland and in Malaysia Cyprus Aden, Kenya – the list, it seems, is endless. How long before it comes out now? What is so strange to me is I never knew I cared until they threw me out. They gave the reason for dumping me, as it was too political for me to carry on. Well, I've got news for them; it is now.

Ignatius looked peeved. I could tell he wished he had come up with something similar.

'You know 'Two and two doesn't make five'. Aren't you making more of this than meets the eye?' Maybe that's not the right saying. But...'

I was getting fed up with him.

'When I first joined the Metropolitan Police force a superior officer once told me, when I challenged him on the validity of one of his arrests, "It doesn't matter whether the suspect was at the scene of the crime or not. What you have to ask yourself is, would they have done it if had been there?"' All these people are now our enemies. We can't screw them legally at this moment in time then we should adopt any means at our disposal to hit back.'

The Priest shook his head; it didn't suit him.

'You are beginning to sound like Al O'Connor yourself, not the rational policeman I thought you were.

'There you go.'

I thanked him. We embraced.

'I am going to Nigeria, you should fly to Hong Kong and apply for a visa for Australia from there.' I haven't seen him since

8. There is one thing more you might like to read

"Okay, I can't guess. I give up. What are we doing here, perched on a hill near Crystal Palace?"

"Patience, I thought this being the last day of our stake-out rota, you deserve an answer."

"It better be good. I was hoping we would slope off and have a celebratory meal."

"I'm not quite sure which one of these houses it is. I know it's on the left-hand side halfway down Hill View Avenue."

"Who told you to come here?"

"Nigel Onobolu. Dick to you."

"What of Tom, Dick and Harry fame?"

"None other."

"Is it going to be Bob Crow's secret hideaway?"

"I saw him on telly the other night. He made sense to me. He said the London Mayor is putting up the Tube fairs, the Railways are cutting staff and raising fares by ten percent. He was organizing a strike ballot. A bloke from the Government said he was causing unnecessary problems. We have all got to tighten our belts and help the country out of the mess that the last Government got us into. Bob Crow just about got it out that it was the greedy bankers' fault before they cut him off."

"You see. We don't have to stake him out, we can watch what he is up to on telly".

"I don't think Jennifer would agree."

"I thought we agreed not to go there."

"There.. Over there..."

"Where?"

"There. In the big bay window, drawing the curtains."

"The one with the light on? Who is it?"

"Auntie Yvonne! If I'm right."

"You're kidding. Aren't you? How come?"

"Nigel Onobolu worked it out. It was Leroy the Flee Man Stuart they buried in Willesden Cemetery on that fateful day."

"Why?"

"Nigel reckons that both John Badger Smith and his team and their mates in the Met had a body on their hands they wanted to hide."

"Why would she agree?"

"Look, she's got a nice house. Nobody from the other side of the River comes this way. Do you remember we had a call from her twin sister I never knew existed? That will be her. No wonder we weren't invited to the funeral. What do you think?"

"I've got nothing more to add. It's a mystery."

"The Smiths would have helped her go, pretending that Leroy Stuart had done her in. When all along it was him they were dumping so they could use his ghost. I wonder how many knew. Was she in trouble? Was someone after her for narking on them? Was she just doing a favour for her patron John Smith?"

"What a selfish old goat, couldn't say goodbye, leave us all wondering. I've got a good mind to go in there and confront her."

"Go on then."

"On second thoughts, best leave her as she is, that way I don't have to have anything to do with her any more. She is dead as far as I am concerned."

"Talking of goats, didn't we promise we would have a steak at McGinty's tonight?'

"Well, I've got my sister baby-sitting and as you don't have anybody to cook for you."

"Why not indeed!"

To be continued…

Lightning Source UK Ltd.
Milton Keynes UK
176247UK00001B/10/P

9 781456 779450

The Devil's Tune

A Vicenda* (A Happening)

Fran Kempton

Chetwynd Books

Published by Chetwynd Books

ISBN printed book: 978-0-9559161-9-9
ISBN e-book: 978-0-9559161-8-2

Cover design by Jessica Bell
Internal design by Polgarus Studio

Chetwynd Books
19 Newport St
Bristol BS3 4ST
UK

For the founding members of BWW.
You know who you are

Part One